BOOK ONE: SHIPWRECK

ISLAND

ATH JU ☒

GORDON KORMAN

BOOK ONE: SHIPWRECK

ISLAND

AN
APPLE
PAPERBACK

SCHOLASTIC INC.
New York Toronto London Auckland Sydney
Mexico City New Delhi Hong Kong Buenos Aires

ISBN 0-439-16456-7

Copyright © 2001 by Gordon Korman.
All rights reserved. Published by Scholastic Inc.
SCHOLASTIC and associated logos are trademarks and/or registered trademarks of Scholastic Inc.

36 35 34 33 32 31 30 29 28 27   3 4 5 6/0

Printed in the U.S.A.   40

First Scholastic printing, June 2001

*For Wayne Turner
Without your help, I would have
been lost at sea.*

*And special thanks to Chris Shields
and "Skipper" Bob Abrams for helping
me find my sea legs.*

BOOK ONE: SHIPWRECK

ISLAND

PROLOGUE
Saturday, July 15, 2010 hours

For a heart-stopping moment, the bow of the *Phoenix* pointed straight up at the boiling black clouds of the storm. Then the wave broke in a cascade of spray, and the schooner was headed down, plummeting into the trough. Shakily, she righted herself and began the long climb up the next thirty-footer.

A streak of forked lightning silhouetted her against white water. She was two-masted, small for a schooner — her deck wasn't much longer than the tallest of the waves. Her sails were down and secured, and she moved under engine power, steered gamely into the oncoming seas.

Suddenly — a flash of white. The mainsail began to rise. It was unthinkable!

No vessel could survive such a storm-carrying sail.

Pandemonium. Angry shouts from the deck. A desperate run for the halyard.

And then the brutal power of the storm filled the half-open sail with violent wind. The ship spun around and heeled over, its twin masts dipping dangerously close to the punishing swells. The

SHIPWRECK

next wave took the *Phoenix* broadside. A torrent washed over the deck.

There might have been a scream when the body hit the water. But the howling of the gale was all that could be heard. . . .

CHAPTER ONE
Sunday, July 9, 2140 hours

Luke Haggerty squeezed into the tiny bathroom and pulled the door shut behind him.

Not the bathroom, he reminded himself. *The head.* Luke knew he'd been sentenced to this boat for the next month. What he didn't know was that it was going to be a never-ending vocabulary lesson. Not walls — *bulkheads.* Not beds — *berths.* The kitchen was a *galley*; a room was a *cabin.* And who cared?

Sudden pounding on the door — was it still called a door?

"What are you doing in there?" growled the voice of Mr. Radford, the *Phoenix*'s first mate. "Writing an opera? Let's go, Archie!"

Luke reached for his belt and bashed his elbow against the small sink. This bathroom — *head* — was a shoe box! "Ow!"

More pounding. "You okay, Archie?"

"My name is Luke."

Even as he said it, he knew it was a waste of breath. All the way from the Guam airport to the marina, Radford had leaned on the horn and cursed out Archie the truck driver, Archie the cop,

SHIPWRECK

4

Archie the pedestrian, Archie the cyclist, and even Archie the priest.

By pressing himself into the corner and resting his left hip against the sink, Luke managed to finish up in the head. He hesitated. The flusher was some kind of pump. Instructions were scribbled on a plastic-coated card tacked to the wall — *bulkhead*: OPEN VALVE, PUMP THREE TIMES, CLOSE VALVE, PUMP THREE TIMES, DUCK.

Duck? Why duck?

Wham! He smacked his head on the low doorway on the way out.

"Watch your head," grunted the mate, not at all better late than never. "Did you remember to close the valve?"

Luke nodded. "What's the big deal?"

"The head flushes with seawater. Last thing you want to do on a boat is let the sea on board. That's a one-way ticket to the bottom."

Luke felt queasy. Ever since he'd learned he was coming here, his uneasy dreams had been a catalog of all the ways to die at sea — hurricanes, tidal waves, giant sharks, and collisions with supertankers, just to name a few. Now he had to add toilets to his list of things to worry about.

"Okay," he sighed. "Where's my cabin?"

Radford brayed a laugh. "You're standing in it, Archie."

"But this is just the — uh — " His voice trailed off. He had been about to say, "The hallway outside the bathroom." But in the dim light, he could make out four narrow bunk beds — bunk berths? — two on either end, and two mini-dressers — all built right into the bulkhead.

"These are your quarters."

"Quarters?" repeated Luke. "As in a quarter of a room?"

"This ain't a luxury liner." Mr. Radford shrugged. "Archie, meet Archie. Lights out at 2200." He heaved himself up the companionway out onto the deck.

Luke cast his eyes around. A tousled head of sandy hair poked out from one of the upper bunks. "What time is it?" Sleepy eyes peered down over rounded, heavily freckled cheeks.

"2145," Luke replied. "I think that's a quarter to twenty-two."

The boy groaned and yawned at the same time. "My system is totally messed up. I was on planes for twenty-one hours to get here."

"Tell me about it," said Luke, beginning to fill a narrow drawer with the contents of his duffel bag. "Why Guam?"

"It's supposed to be just us and the ocean," replied the other boy. "No ports, no nothing. The brochure said we probably won't even see another boat for the whole month." He sounded mournful, like it was a death sentence.

Luke applied a hip-check to the overstuffed drawer. "Nobody showed me any brochure."

"Really?" The boy was surprised. "How'd you end up here?"

The horrible movie replayed itself in Luke's head as it had so many times before. The crack of the judge's gavel; that single word: *guilty*; his mother's tears. And later, in the judge's chambers: "I'm reluctant to sentence a thirteen-year-old to Williston, especially on a first offense. There's one other possibility. It's a program called CNC — Charting a New Course. . . ."

Luke cast his roommate a strange smile. "I'm a convicted felon." He held out his hand. "Luke Haggerty."

"Wow!" The boy's eyes widened. "I'm only here because I fight with my sister. I'm Will," he added, shaking hands. "Will Greenfield."

"Fight with your sister?" Luke raised an eyebrow. "So your parents had to put an ocean between you?"

"Nah, she's in the girls' cabin next door. I guarantee you'll hate her. I should have been an only child."

Luke laughed shortly. "I *am* an only child.

It doesn't help. If you don't have any brothers and sisters, your parents are on your case extra."

The lights flashed once and winked out. Except for the dim glow from the porthole, the cabin was in total darkness.

"Well, I guess I've decided to go to sleep," Luke said sarcastically. He established himself on the lower bed — bunk — *berth!* — on the opposite side of the room. Uncomfortably, he curled up in the coolest spot he could find.

For a few minutes, the only sound that could be heard was the creaking of the mooring lines and the soft lapping of water against the hull. Then —

"What felony?" Will asked.

Luke laughed without humor. "Not murder, if that's what you're worried about."

But even as he said it, the voice of the prosecutor was ringing in his ears: "Felony possession of a firearm."

"Come on," coaxed Will. "I told you why *I'm* here. What was it? Breaking and entering? Vandalism? I know — assault!"

"That'll be my *next* felony," yawned Luke, "if I ever get my hands on the kid who put that gun in my locker."

SHIPWRECK

CHAPTER TWO
Monday, July 10, 0820 hours

Captain James Cascadden had a rugged leathery face that looked like it had been rubbed against every coral reef in the seven seas. He was six-foot-five, so he had to duck through the tight hatches and companionways of the *Phoenix*. But the movement was so natural, almost graceful, that Luke had the impression that the man had been born and lived his entire sixty-plus years on boats like this one.

Captain Cascadden hated long speeches, except when he was the person giving them. "None of you came to me because you want to learn the ways of the sea." His voice was a deep bass with the rich tone of a bassoon. "Many of you are from troubled backgrounds, some including difficulties with the law." A flash of penetrating eyes. "Aboard this ship, all that means nothing. The slate is clean. I don't care about who you are now. All that matters is who you *will be* — a crew. My crew. And together we will serve this vessel. Join me, and we'll sail off to adventure."

"Like I've got a choice," Luke mumbled under his breath.

ISLAND

Mr. Radford was there to keep the audience in line. "Shut up, Archie! When the captain talks, only the captain is talking!"

The first "adventure" turned out to be swabbing the deck. Luke found himself mopping and fuming. Only three of the six crew members had arrived for the trip. How fair was it for half the people to do all the work?

He slaved alongside Will, listening to his bunk mate bicker with his sister, Lyssa.

"Why are you mopping *there*? I already did that part!"

"Yeah? That's why it needs doing again!"

Luke smiled in spite of himself. Will and Lyssa were such opposites of each other that it almost made sense that they didn't get along. He was husky; she was skinny. His face was round; hers was angular. His eyes seldom left the deck and the job at hand; she seemed bright and fascinated by everything that was going on around her. She watched the captain and Radford, and even Luke, with a friendly interest.

"I hear you're a felon," she said cheerfully.

Luke's face flamed red. The Greenfields may have hated each other, but they obviously didn't mind sharing a little gossip. "It's a long story," he muttered.

"We almost got a criminal record once,"

SHIPWRECK

she went on, "but our lawyer got the charges dropped when we promised not to do it again."

"Hey!" Mr. Radford called from partway up the mast, where he was adjusting some rigging. "Less talk and more work, Archie! Same to you, Veronica!"

Well, that explained where the names came from. Mr. Radford was a reader of fine literature — comic books.

Luke turned back to where brother and sister were snapping at each other. This family was some piece of work. Real funny to joke about criminal records to a guy who had one that would never go away. Like you could get arrested for sibling squabbles, anyway. What kind of nut-job parents would send their kids halfway around the world just because they argue like every other brother and sister on the planet?

And then it happened. One second they were bickering. The next, Lyssa cocked back her mop and took a home-run swing at her brother's head, missing by half an inch. It was that fast. Luke blinked and almost missed it.

In a split second, Radford was out of the rigging and poised between them. "If you two want to kill each other, don't do it on my watch!"

And then they were back to their work as if nothing had happened.

Maniacs, thought Luke. *I'm surrounded by maniacs.*

The job of swabbing was short, if not sweet. For a sixty-foot boat, there was practically nowhere to stand on the *Phoenix.* The whole center of the vessel housed the system of sails and the masts, booms, lines, and rigging that supported it. The cockpit and main cabin top took up most of the aft space. The sleeping quarters dominated the forward part of the boat, with the galley and cargo hatch toward the middle — *amidships.* So all that was left to walk on was a thin path of deck ringing the schooner and a couple of very tight cut-throughs between the masts. Equipment was piled on every surface — poles, fenders, anchors, the *Phoenix's* twelve-foot dinghy, and what seemed like enough rope to stretch across any ocean. In a way, it was brilliant, Luke thought. There was room for everything — everything except people. Surely even Williston provided more space for its inmates. An only child who had never even shared a bedroom, he could almost feel the squeeze in his gut. The idea of living on this floating sardine can made him shudder.

In addition to being the first mate and the warden, Mr. Radford was also ship's cook. At lunch in the tiny galley, he proved that he could open a tin of baked beans as well as any of the great chefs of Europe.

While cooking was the mate's job, cleaning up and washing dishes turned out to be just another part of the adventure. The galley was ventilated only by a small smoke-head on the cabin top. It seemed twice as hot as the rest of the boat — as the rest of Guam, for that matter. Luke and Will did the work in sweaty silence. Talking just didn't seem to be worth the effort.

After lunch, Mr. Radford headed to the airport to meet a plane, and the three crew members were given a tour of the cockpit.

"Now, what's the most important instrument here?" asked Captain Cascadden.

"The wheel?" suggested Will.

"Of course not," snapped Lyssa testily. "How about the radio?"

"That's downstairs in the navigation room, *stupid!*" Will snapped.

"Not 'downstairs,' " the captain amended. "On shipboard we say 'below.' "

"How about the compass?" suggested Lyssa brightly. If her brother's constant attacks bothered her, she didn't show it. *Probably,* thought Luke, *because she didn't have a mop in her hand.*

"All those are important," the captain agreed. "But," his hand touched a small, ordinary-looking switch on the instrument panel, "this is more important than all of them. This is the blower switch. It turns on the fan that airs out the engine room. Never, ever start the engine of a boat without starting the blower first. Otherwise, fuel vapors that have built up there could explode when the engine ignites." He stared at them with burning black eyes. "If you forget everything else you learn here, remember this one thing."

That turned out to be a favorite line of Captain Cascadden's. Like when he told the group that a boat does not respond immediately to a turn of the wheel. "It's not like your bicycle that goes where you tell it when you tell it. An inexperienced helmsman will oversteer because he keeps on turning until he feels his ship change direction. If you forget everything else you learn here, remember this one thing."

He also said it about storing ropes and lines in a coiled position to keep them straight and ready to use, tying the sails down in a storm, and even cleaning up the sleeping quarters.

Captain Cascadden pointed ashore. "Oh, look, here's Mr. Radford, bringing us two more crew members. It's important to make the newcomers feel welcome."

"And if you forget everything else," Luke whispered to Will, "remember this one thing."

SHIPWRECK

Will covered up a snicker with some coughing.

The two new arrivals looked terrible, but a lot of that could have been the daylong flights. Charla Swann seemed to be about Luke's age. She was tall and rail-thin and moved like a cat. There was a no-nonsense look to her. Her hair was plain, her clothes were simple. Her appearance was engineered for efficiency rather than show. Ian Sikorsky was at least a couple of years younger. The slight boy with sad eyes was already embroiled in a battle with Radford over his luggage. The mate had removed a sleek laptop computer with wireless modem, and Ian seemed ready to try to swim home rather than part with it.

Soon the captain got himself in the middle of it. "Crewman, Charting a New Course is about casting off your old life for a new and better one."

"But what about the Internet?" the boy asked plaintively.

"We have our own Internet out here," Cascadden assured him. "It's called teamwork. A ship and her crew, coming together to form a web of comradeship and cooperation. What electronic gadget could give you that?"

Radford put it less poetically. "No computers, Archie. CNC rules. It goes home UPS — PDQ."

Ian looked so miserable that he barely raised his head as he walked up the gangway onto the deck.

"Hey, Ian," Luke said kindly, "when you see our room, you'll be happy it had to go. We need all the space we can get."

"Well, Mr. Radford," Captain Cascadden said cheerfully, "that's our whole load, then?"

"One more, skipper," the mate replied.

The captain frowned. "Now, how could that be? There aren't any more flights due in."

"This isn't your regular Archie," said Radford. "This kid's coming by private jet."

CHAPTER THREE
Monday, July 10, 1805 hours

As soon as the door of the Learjet opened, J.J. Lane's one-of-a-kind designer sunglasses fogged up with the oppressive blast of Guam humidity.

"Whoa! Aloha!" the fourteen-year-old chortled, handing the glasses over to his traveling companion, Dan Rapaport, for cleaning.

Rapaport was personal assistant to the world-famous movie star Jonathan Lane, J.J.'s father. Lately, though, it seemed like his new job was as the keeper of J.J., who had turned into a real Hollywood brat.

"Aloha is what they say in Hawaii," Rapaport told his charge. "I don't know what they say here."

J.J. shrugged. "Doesn't matter." He hopped down to the tarmac. "Where's my luggage?"

Rapaport permitted himself a secret smile as he handed over a small duffel bag.

"No, really," J.J. insisted. "There's half a dozen suitcases in the cargo hold."

Rapaport shook his head. "We left those when we stopped in Honolulu."

"On *purpose?*"

ISLAND

"CNC gave us a list, J.J., and it didn't say anything about hang gliders."

The movie star's son folded his arms across his chest. "I'm not going."

"Suit yourself," said Rapaport. "But you're not coming back with me. Have a nice month on Guam. And — oh, yeah — I canceled your credit cards."

J.J.'s reaction was equal parts shock and fury. "I'm calling Dad!" He pulled out his cell phone and dialed furiously. He listened for a moment, then threw the phone down to the pavement. "My service has been terminated."

"You're lucky. It's midnight in L.A. right now. I doubt your father would be thrilled to hear from you." Rapaport took a deep breath. "Listen, J.J., when you brought a case of champagne to the eighth-grade dance, I worked hard to keep it out of the papers. When you sold the video of your father's pool party to *Entertainment Tonight*, I covered for you. When you did all that upscale shoplifting on Rodeo Drive, it was me who arranged for your father to make that donation to the Policeman's Brotherhood Fund. But when you took your father's Harley and drove it through the plate-glass window of that art gallery — that's when it became time to get out of town for a while."

SHIPWRECK

"Out of town means Santa Barbara — maybe even Tahoe. Not *Mars!*"

"You're a flake, J.J.," said Rapaport, "but you're not an idiot. Even you can see that these little happenings of yours are getting worse and worse. You're going to kill somebody one of these days — maybe even yourself."

The boy wrinkled his nose. "You're enjoying this, aren't you?"

A wide grin split Rapaport's face. "Oh, yeah." He noticed the CNC logo on the hat of the man striding across the tarmac toward them. "This must be Mr. Radford now." He turned to the sailor and held out his hand. "I'm Dan Rapaport from Jonathan Lane's office."

Radford brushed right past him and took the duffel bag from J.J. "Okay, Richie Rich. We sail in an hour."

Totally ignored, Rapaport withdrew his hand. For a brief instant, he looked like he wanted to rescue J.J. from his fate. Then he remembered the art gallery window and the Picasso with the tire treads on it. He got back in the Learjet and pulled the door shut behind him.

CHAPTER FOUR
Tuesday, July 11, 0730 hours

"Heave!" bellowed Mr. Radford, untying the lines and pitching them onto the *Phoenix*.

Luke, Charla, and Lyssa stood on the edge of the deck, poles in hand, pushing against the dock to move the schooner away from its mooring.

"Put some back into it!" howled the mate.

Luke strained until he felt his spine was about to snap. Water opened up between dock and boat. Radford jumped on board. He cupped his hands to his mouth.

"Clear!"

In the cockpit, Captain Cascadden engaged the engine. The *Phoenix* began to pick her way delicately out of the harbor.

Luke watched the multicolored sails of the other boats go by as the deck thrummed under his feet. Sure, he would have given his right arm to be almost anywhere else. But there was a certain majesty to gliding across the water — definitely a feeling you couldn't get in Williston Juvenile Detention Facility. He could see that his fellow crew members felt it too — all except one.

"Captain, my father is a powerful man in Hol-

SHIPWRECK

lywood," said J.J. smoothly. "I know he'd make it worth your while if you put me on a plane back to the States."

The captain's eyes never wavered from the course he was steering. "This *is* the States, crewman."

"You know — the *real* States. L.A."

"Coast Guard cutter off the starboard bow, three hundred yards!" warned Radford from his perch on the ratlines.

"Your father," said the captain, "paid good money for you to be on this trip. I saw the check, crewman."

"It's a misunderstanding," J.J. insisted. "He signed me up for the boat thing, just not *this* boat thing. I mean, no offense, but you've got four people sleeping in a closet! And the bathroom is a phone booth! I can't even — "

HONK!!

Will clamped himself onto a bulwark and held on until the earsplitting blast of the air horn died away. His racing heart slowed. What was he doing here? How had his life come to this — on the wrong side of the globe, setting sail on a wooden cracker box?

If I get out of this, he made a deal with the sky, *I swear I'll never cheat on another math test.*

The *Phoenix* didn't put on the brakes and turn

around. Instead, the schooner eased through the mouth of the harbor.

So he sweetened the pot. *I swear I'll floss from now on. Every night!*

Rough hands grabbed him by the collar. "Off your butt, Archie! This is a working ship!" Radford cupped his hands to his mouth. "Ready on the mainsail, Skipper!"

"Haul!" bellowed the captain.

Will and Charla began yanking away at the halyard, hand over hand. With a creak of the rigging, the mainsail began to rise.

Ahead of them, Luke and Ian were hauling up the foresail, their faces taut with concentration.

Closer to the bow, J.J. and Lyssa worked on the smaller staysail.

Didn't it figure? They gave Lyssa the easy sail. It had been like that from the beginning. She was always the sweet little baby, while Will was the older one who should know better. People loved Lyssa. The good looks in the family were all hers; he got stuck with freckles. She was a straight-A student; he struggled.

"I should have been an only child," he grunted through the strain of his effort.

Charla looked down at him like he was crazy — Lyssa's fault as usual.

When the wind caught the half-open mainsail,

its force pulled the halyard right out of Will's hand, delivering a painful rope burn. Charla held on, but with the sail taut, the line was difficult to budge. Will clamped himself on again, and both leaned into it with all their might. Up went the sail, flapping full.

"You'll earn your dinner tonight!" roared Radford. The mate had joined Luke and Ian. Soon the foresail was up.

Last came the jibs, two small sails extended from the head of the foremast to the bowsprit — the long thin spar that stretched forward from the bow.

The crew fell back, exhausted.

Will looked down at his hands, which were blistered and bleeding. You'd think they'd figure out a way to put up sails without taking off all your skin!

He caught sight of his sister. She was smiling! *Smiling!*

If this is over really fast, Will promised, *I swear I'll get in shape! I'll jog every day! I'll lift weights! I'll —*

"Don't get comfortable!" bawled Radford. "This is the mainsheet! It's not a sheet off your bed; it's a line. And these pulleys are called blocks. Watch what happens when I ease up on the mainsheet."

Expertly, the mate undid the knot and gave the rope some slack. He turned to Luke. "Hey, Archie — "

Luke turned. "Yeah?"

A gust of wind took the sail and swung it out over their heads at right angles to the boat.

Bang! The block swept around and smacked Luke full in the face, knocking him off his feet.

Radford laughed out loud. "I was going to warn you, but never mind."

When the foresail was aligned, Captain Cascadden cut power and let the schooner run with the wind. The crisp ocean breeze blew away the stifling Guam humidity in an instant.

"Now you're sailing!" rumbled the captain behind the wheel. "There's no feeling quite like it!"

Lyssa hopped up on the engine housing, threw her arms wide, and let her long hair whip in the wind. "Feel that breeze!"

"Where I come from," Charla told her, "a wind like this would knock you right off the fire escape!"

Will burned. Lyssa was making friends here like she did everywhere. By the time this trip was over, she was going to be voted Miss Congeniality on this tub. This would be like a vacation for her while he suffered.

It was so unfair. If it wasn't for Lyssa, they wouldn't even be on this dumb trip! Sure, he got in her face a lot. She deserved it. Besides, when they were fighting, it was always Lyssa who went ballistic.

Involuntarily, his mind jumped to the incident that his parents had come to call The Last Straw. The argument started out small — two Halloween parties, who would get dropped off first, something like that. No big deal.

He remembered Mom in the background, screaming for them to calm down. And then the marble rolling pin from Lyssa's chef's costume was hurtling toward his face. He heard, rather than felt, his nose break. The blood poured like somebody had busted a hydrant. He couldn't even recall fighting back. He must have, though. Because when he woke up in the hospital, Lyssa was in the next bed with a concussion. Both of them were so beaten up that the cops had to file a special report to rule out child abuse.

"Take my word for it," the officer assured the Greenfield parents. "If you don't do something about these two, they're going to kill each other."

And — just their luck! — the admitting nurse happened to have a third cousin whose juvenile delinquent son had been sent on a boat trip called Charting a New Course.

Tears stung Will's eyes as Guam became smaller and smaller. Oh, great! Now he was going to be ship's crybaby too!

He ran for the companionway to the main cabin, determined that no one should see him.

There he came face-to-face with Luke, who was holding a cold towel to his rapidly swelling eye.

"You're my witness!" Luke seethed. "You saw that lousy Rat-face! He did it on purpose!"

Will smiled, his first of the day. "Rat-face Radford. Why didn't I think of that? That's funny."

"No, it isn't," Luke raged. "It's the least funny thing on a very unfunny trip!"

With a sigh, Will followed him back on deck. It was some small comfort that he wasn't the only one who was miserable.

Lyssa was hanging around the captain, schmoozing him while he explained how the boat's motor worked.

Will snorted in disgust. One science fair project on the internal combustion engine and Lyssa thought she was Jeff Gordon's whole pit crew.

He looked back to the sky. *If I get out of this —*

But he wasn't getting out of anything. Guam was barely a speck on the horizon. The best he could hope for was a sign. Something — anything — that hinted all this might turn out okay.

An odd look came over Lyssa's face as she stood with the captain halfway down the engine hatch. With a strangled sound, she scrambled to the side, draped herself over the lifeline, and was thoroughly, violently sick.

CHAPTER FIVE
Wednesday, July 12, 1100 hours

Lyssa hit the water first, a cannonball that sent a splash all the way back to Captain Cascadden in the cockpit.

"It's *warm!*" she shrieked, amazed.

Will was next, climbing carefully down the boat's swim ladder. He submerged and bobbed like a cork. "It *is* warm! It's great!"

Luke jumped in and paddled around happily. It felt good to be cool and clean.

"Hey, Ian," called Will. "Come get your feet wet."

The younger boy averted his eyes. "I don't think so."

"Come on! You'll love it!" Lyssa promised.

But Ian had disappeared down the companionway to the sleeping quarters.

Luke shook his head. "Poor kid. He forgot to download his personality before they made him ship his computer home."

"I wonder why he got sent here," mused Lyssa.

"He probably wouldn't mind his own business, just like you," snickered Will.

"Shut up."

Charla stood poised on the gunwale. She was perched only on the tips of her toes, but she didn't move a muscle, even with the gentle rocking of the boat. Gracefully, she sailed off the side in a perfect jackknife, hitting the water with barely a splash.

The other swimmers and even Captain Cascadden burst into cheers and applause.

Charla broke the surface, took a few smooth powerful strokes, then flipped effortlessly to float on her back. She had always been comfortable in the water, but it was more than that. Swimming somehow seemed to relieve her pressures and tensions, and she had quite a few.

"You're a fish!" cried Will.

She shrugged modestly. "I'm on the swim team at school."

"And the diving team?" asked Luke.

She nodded shyly.

"But you were talking about track and field before," put in Lyssa.

"Only the hundred meters and the hurdles," said Charla, embarrassed by the attention. "I like gymnastics better, anyway." She felt a twinge of uneasiness. Why was she talking so much? These people didn't need to know her private business.

"Man, what are you doing *here*?" exclaimed

Luke. "You're the perfect kid! What — your parents signed you up because you're too good? Maybe you can take rotten lessons from Ratface."

Charla's smile disappeared. "I'm not so good." In two textbook strokes, she was at the ladder and clambering back on board.

Luke was mystified. "What'd I say?"

"Don't worry, Luke," said Will. "You can accuse me of being good. I can take it."

Lyssa splashed him in the face. "There are a lot of words that describe you. Good isn't one of them."

Charla glared down at them from the gunwale. Rich kids always acted like they knew everything. What did they have to worry about, besides deciding which mall to shop at? The other athletes she knew — the ones whose dads weren't working three jobs — could enjoy their sports. It wasn't their ticket.

"It's your ticket out, Charla. . . . It's your ticket up. . . . Your ticket to college . . . Your ticket to a better life."

She heard those words twenty times a day from her father. "Pick one sport. You're spreading yourself too thin. It's your ticket to the Olympic team. Go, go, go."

I'm twelve, Dad. And isn't this supposed to be

*fun? I don't want a ticket. If I even hear the word
again, I'm going to scream!*

Maybe if she'd had the guts to say that, she
might have avoided that fateful morning when
she couldn't get out of bed because her arms
and legs wouldn't move. Charla Swann, who
could twist herself into a graceful pretzel on the
uneven bars, could barely walk into the emergency room. And yet there was nothing physi-
cally wrong with her.

"Burnout. Classic burnout," the doctor had
said.

And that had led to a *ticket* even her father
hadn't anticipated — the one to Guam that included a berth on the *Phoenix* with a bunch of
spoiled rich kids.

Well, okay, they weren't *really* rich. Just richer
than her, which wasn't hard to be. Except for that
hotshot from California. He was loaded. He had
a pair of sunglasses that would probably sell for
more than her dad's car.

Come to think of it, where *was* J.J.?

And then a voice yelled, "Aloha!"

A voice from *above*. There was J.J., high up
in the mainsail rigging.

Captain Cascadden saw him too. "Crewman
— get down from there *this instant!*"

J.J. waved. "Sorry, Captain! Can't hear you!"

"Mr. Radford!" roared the captain. "I need you on deck!"

The mate was asleep in his berth, after taking last night's watch. But the captain's strident voice brought him up the companionway in a matter of seconds. He took in the scene in an instant.

"Don't even think about it!" he barked furiously.

Too late. With a cry of *"Geronimo!"* J.J. grabbed onto a loose rope and swung himself off the mainmast, clear past the deck and out over the open sea. There he let go and dropped like a stone into the water.

It seemed like a long time — a breathless time — before J.J. surfaced again, howling in triumph. The celebration was short-lived.

Cursing with rage, Mr. Radford took a running leap off the side of the boat and hit the water swimming. His form was crude and untrained, but Charla had never seen anybody move that fast in water. He scooped J.J. up Red Cross style, towed him back to the swim ladder, and hauled him, still protesting, on board.

"You miserable little muckworm, do you know what mutiny is?"

J.J. blinked innocently. "Wasn't that a classic movie from way back when you were — you know — still old?"

SHIPWRECK

Now Radford was screaming. "Listen, Richie Rich! When we left Guam, we left the United States! In international waters, the captain is God! And I'm assistant God! When we say come down, down is where you come!"

He turned his fury on the three still in the water. "Okay, swimming's over! You've got your friend Richie Rich to thank for that!"

Charla watched in sympathy as Luke, Will, and Lyssa scrambled nervously up the swim ladder. Captain Cascadden was a nice man, she reflected, but he didn't seem to notice that his mate was more than just a gruff sailor. Mr. Radford didn't like people, especially kids. And his bullying seemed to increase with their distance from land.

She swallowed hard. They were going a lot farther than this. . . .

CHAPTER SIX
Thursday, July 13, 2235 hours

Luke had plenty of complaints about shipboard life, but he couldn't say there was nothing to do. In fact, he'd never been so busy. The sails alone were a full-time career. They constantly needed raising, lowering, trimming, letting in, letting out — somehow, the state they were in was never the right one.

When Luke and the others weren't fussing with the boat, they were fussing with the sea around it. Science stuff, mostly. Whale watching, plankton tows, identifying schools of fish. They did math with wave heights and water temperatures and indexed it to their location, which they got from the handheld global positioning satellite system.

It was all supposed to go in their logbooks, but Luke could never think of anything to write. He was sitting on deck, trying to describe a fish he'd seen ten hours ago, when a shadow fell across the flash-lit page.

Captain Cascadden was unfolding his six-foot-five frame out of the companionway. "Evening, crewman." He noticed the logbook in

Luke's hand. "Ah, keeping a log is one of the great pleasures of life at sea. As the years go by, you'll read this over many times."

Right. Like he wanted to relive this lousy trip any more than he wanted to remember the arrest and trial leading up to it. But he bit his tongue and said nothing. Captain Cascadden could be annoying with his long, boring speeches about the joys of the sea. But he was a nice guy at heart. You definitely had to respect him. Not like Rat-face.

"Here's something that would make a fascinating entry," the captain rambled on, pointing to the sky. "Notice the bright halo around the moon. According to legend, that tells of a coming storm. Count the stars inside the ring — one, two. That means the storm is two days away."

"Really?" Luke was amazed. "And that works?"

The captain chuckled. "It's just an old salt's tale. But a hundred years ago, it was considered science." He made a great show of lighting a corncob pipe. "Today we get constant weather updates by fax."

"So there's no storm," said Luke.

"We're fine," the captain assured him. "Rougher seas tomorrow, though. No swimming."

Luke said good night and slipped down the companionway to the boys' cabin.

"Bad news, Evel Knievel," he said to J.J. "No swimming tomorrow. You'll have to find another way to kill yourself."

"Bug off," yawned the actor's son. He rolled over in his bunk and banged on the bulkhead. "Hey, ladies, which one of you wants to come over and give me a nice foot massage?" There was a scrambling sound on deck above them, followed by the shuffling of shoes on the companionway.

The furious face of Mr. Radford soon appeared. "Hey, Richie Rich. The girls' cabin is on the starboard side. Behind this bulkhead is where I sleep. And if I get any more invitations like that, you're going over the side with an anchor in your pants."

"Way to go," Luke muttered in a low voice as the mate stormed away. "Rat-face isn't the friendliest guy in the world as it is. Thanks for putting him in an even worse mood. We really need the grief."

"It's not smart," added Will in a softer tone. "When he's mad at you, he's mad at all of us."

"Thanks for the life lessons," said J.J. sarcastically. "Don't you know who I am? My father is Jonathan Lane!"

"And I'm Bugs Bunny's kid," snorted Luke. "Notice the family resemblance?"

"I *am*!" J.J. insisted. He pulled his sunglasses out of his shirt pocket. "Paul Smith, the fashion designer, gave these to my dad in England last year. They're custom-made. There's not another pair exactly like them in the world!"

Luke examined the sleek silver shades. On one earpiece was engraved: JONATHAN LANE, THE TOAST OF LONDON — P.S.

Will was impressed. "Your dad's an amazing actor."

It all came together in Luke's mind — rich father, fancy lawyers. If Luke had had that . . .

"This is just great!" he exclaimed. "You're allowed to be a maniac because you know your big-shot daddy has the power to get you out of anything!"

Furious, J.J. leaped out of his bunk and leaned into Luke's face. "Well, I'm stuck here with you! So obviously there are a few things he can't get me out of, right?"

They stood seething, toe-to-toe.

"Hey, come on — " began Will. But a brawl seemed unavoidable.

And then a muffled sob broke through the tension. All three turned to follow the sound.

Ian Sikorsky rocked back and forth on his

bunk. His knees pulled into his chest, he was crying as if he had just met the end of the world.

"Hey," said Luke in a voice that was none too steady. "Don't do that. Nothing's worth it."

"Yeah," echoed J.J., speaking as much to Luke as to Ian.

Ian nodded and sniffled, struggling to get himself under control.

It was Will who couldn't leave well enough alone. "Ian, what did a nice kid like you do to get yourself a seat on this Windjammer cruise?"

"I — I watched TV," quavered the younger boy, and the tears started up again. This time there was no stopping them until sleep claimed him.

SHIPWRECK

CHAPTER SEVEN
Friday, July 14, 0610 hours

Slam!

Four orange life jackets came sailing down to the deck of the crew quarters.

Will came awake with a start. He sat up and was nearly tossed from his berth by the rolling of the cabin.

"Personal floatation devices!" barked Mr. Radford. "Get dressed and get in them!"

Will's heart was in his throat. "Is the boat sinking?"

"They're called waves!" snarled the mate. "Maybe you've heard of them. Now hurry up!"

The four boys got themselves ready in a tangle of elbows and knees. On deck, they found Lyssa on her hands and knees at the gunwale, throwing up over the side.

It was the one sight that could have brought a smile to Will's gray face. "Mom and Dad always tell us: Find what you do best and do your best with it. You're turning into a real whiz at barfing, Lyss."

Lyssa was too weak to fire off a retort.

"Good morning!" bellowed the captain from

ISLAND

the cockpit. "I think today might test your sea legs a little. We're seeing eight-foot waves with swells in the ten-foot range. And the wind's going to pick up later in the day. So let's be extra careful on deck. Now I want all of you to go and eat a hearty breakfast. You'll need your strength. That's all."

The six crew members crept gingerly aft and climbed down the companionway to the tiny galley, which was just off the main cabin. There the powerful odor of sizzling butter practically knocked them over.

"Scrambled eggs!" crowed Mr. Radford. "Nice and greasy! They'll slide all the way down!"

In a flash, Lyssa was back up on deck, gulping air.

Luke opened the latch and folded the table down from the bulkhead. The crew gathered around it.

"That Rat-face is some piece of work," he muttered. "Three days of dry toast, but now that we've hit heavy seas, he decides to get creative in the kitchen!"

It was a rough day on the inexperienced crew. The wind was whipping around the rigging, and the deck pitched to and fro. They struggled through the fine chilling spray off the whitecaps, their shoes slipping on the slick deck. By 1100 hours, Will was beside his sister at the rail, giving up his scrambled eggs to the Pacific.

"It's days like this," yowled Mr. Radford, "that made me become a sailor!"

The *Phoenix* tacked, sailing close-hauled at an angle, first to port, then to starboard.

"It's called beating to windward," the captain explained. "We can get where we're going in a zigzag without ever having to sail into the wind."

The constant changes in direction meant a lot of work on the sails. Their hands were raw and bleeding by the time Mr. Radford called lunch.

The meal was another rough-weather master-piece — liver and onions with canned succotash. The mate took great delight in watching the faces turn green. Ian and J.J. barely touched their food, but Luke refused to give Radford the satisfaction of hearing him say uncle. He sat across the table from the cook, glaring into his eyes, and match-ing him mouthful for mouthful.

"Ready for seconds?" challenged the mate.

"Bring it on," replied Luke, tight-lipped.

The wind got stronger. Captain Cascadden ordered the sails trimmed and took down the two jibs on the bowsprit. By this time, the swells were reaching twelve feet.

"It's like a roller coaster!" moaned Will, hugging the mainsheet as if he were trying to enmesh himself in the ropes and pulleys.

If I get through this day, he vowed, *I swear I'll give up smoking if I ever start!*

"I love the sea!" roared Mr. Radford, shaking off a faceful of spray like a sheepdog after a bath. "We'll make sailors of you lot yet!"

"I'm a landlubber," J.J. groaned defensively. "And the more time I spend on this boat, the more I lub the land."

Luke had never seen the mate this happy. Rat-face was so nasty that it took everybody's combined misery to put him in a good mood.

"Hey, Archie," he called to Luke. "You don't look so hot. You'll feel a lot better if you let that seasickness out."

Luke grimaced. His stomach was doing serious backflips. That would put the crowning touch on Rat-face's day.

He set his jaw. It was never going to happen. Grim with determination, he staggered forward, stumbled down the companionway, and squeezed himself into the tiny head. He couldn't even get down on his knees — there wasn't enough room. He just bent over the bowl and surrendered to his overwhelming nausea.

Then he flushed away all traces, rinsed out his mouth, and washed his face.

SHIPWRECK

Back on deck, the captain was addressing the assembled crew. "There's no break from these rough seas yet. We're going to have to strike the sails and heave to under power."

"I heaved already," said J.J. feelingly.

"Shut up, Richie Rich!" snapped Radford. " 'Heave to' means turning into the wind. If you listen, you might hear what you don't hear because you're not listening!"

"Captain," said Will in a timid voice, "how scared should we be? I mean — are we in trouble here?"

The captain threw back his head and laughed heartily. "Steady on, my boy, this is an ordinary day at the office for the *Phoenix*. She's been in seas twice this size and come through with flying colors. She's a fine ship, seaworthy in every way."

So down came the sails.

No one felt like eating. But the captain ordered toast and ginger ale for all hands. The swells were reaching fifteen feet. Standing near the bow, it looked as if the sea were opening up to swallow the *Phoenix*. The troughs between waves were so low that, for a second, there was dead calm down there — no wind, no spray. It was the eeriest part. Luke actually found himself yearning for the blustery chaos atop the crests.

Ian was the first to decide to ride out the rough seas strapped into his bunk. He disappeared down the companionway. A moment later there was a bloodcurdling scream.

"We're sinking! *We're sinking!*"

Mr. Radford ran over to the companionway. "Take it easy, Archie. We're not sinking." He looked down and saw the boy standing up to his ankles in water. "Holy — Skipper, we've got water in the crew cabin!"

Captain Cascadden turned on the bilge pump and grabbed the person closest to him. "Crewman, take the wheel!"

Will stared at him in shock and horror. "But I don't know how to drive!"

"We're in the open Pacific," the captain assured him. "You're not going to hit anything. Just hold her steady. I'll be right back."

Will stood there with an iron grip on the wheel. The captain hurried below.

"A leak?" he asked his mate.

"Negative."

Lyssa jumped down the companionway to the girls' quarters. "No water in here, Captain!" she called.

Captain Cascadden opened the door to the head. Eight inches of water poured out into the cabin. The toilet bowl was full and overflowing.

Seawater surged out of the flusher pump with each wave that hit the boat.

The captain reached down and twisted the lever on the pump. "False alarm, Mr. Radford. Somebody forgot to close the valve."

"I'll kill him!" threatened the mate.

"You'll do no such thing," chuckled the captain. "In fact, I don't even want to know who it was. Get a pump and bail out this cabin."

A bell went off in Luke's mind. He pictured himself sick as a dog but determined that Rat-face would never find out about his Technicolor yawn. He'd put so much energy into cleaning up the evidence that he'd forgotten to shut the valve.

Guiltily, he volunteered for the worst job in the pumping operation. His pants rolled up to his knees, he stood in the head, holding the sucking tube and trying not to fall in the toilet as the deck tossed under his feet.

Mr. Radford ranted through the whole business. "How many times do I have to tell you to close *that valve*? Does anybody have half a brain on this ship?"

It was torture, Luke thought. But it was better than having to confess that all this was his fault.

CHAPTER EIGHT
Saturday, July 15, 0650 hours

J.J. Lane was dreaming about bikinis. The pool deck was packed with them.

"You must be an actress," he said to a yellow one with stars on it.

The girl reached out to him and . . .

Smack!

Will Greenfield's arm came down off the upper bunk, and the open hand slapped J.J. full in the face.

The actor's son sat bolt upright, visions of swimsuits popping like soap bubbles before his bleary eyes. Bright sunshine shone down the companionway. He checked his Rolex watch, a birthday gift from Madonna. 6:53.

Huh? Radford usually had them up by six. He heard the deep rumble of the captain's voice above them.

"Let them sleep, Mr. Radford. They were pretty sick yesterday and they need their rest. You and I can get these sails up."

Radford laughed. "Sure can, Skipper. And we'll have an easier time of it than they do."

J.J. heard the captain chuckle. Then he heard

SHIPWRECK

another sound — a power hum, and the scrape and squeak of a mechanical winch in operation.

Frowning, he crept up the companionway and peered out on deck. The captain and mate were both in the cockpit. And the mainsail was rising — *all by itself!*

He let himself drop to the deck of the cabin. "Unbelievable!"

The other three boys stirred.

"More trouble?" Will asked fearfully.

J.J. was so angry he could barely speak. "The captain and Radford — they're raising sails!"

Luke climbed down from his bunk. "Just so long as we don't have to do it."

"They're raising sails *automatically!*" J.J. exclaimed. "There's a gizmo in the cockpit that does it like a garage door opener!"

Ian spoke up. "You mean all that halyard work — ?"

"For nothing," confirmed the actor's son. "They could have done it with the touch of a button — like they're doing *this minute!*"

"Those jerks," Luke muttered. "I'll bet Rat-face is laughing inside every time we rip up our hands hauling those ropes."

"It's probably CNC's policy — you know, learning teamwork by doing everything the old-fashioned way," Will put in.

"By suffering," Luke added.

"We can't let them get away with this," J.J. said, tight-lipped.

"What can we do about it?" asked Ian. "They're in charge, and we're not. We have to do what they say."

"We can fight back," J.J. insisted.

Luke glared at him. "I don't like CNC, but it's better than jail — and that's where I go if I don't complete this trip! Don't even *think* about messing it up for me."

Will struggled into his life jacket and pulled the straps tight around his back. That was the fourth time. Six more to go, Radford's orders. Yesterday, Will had spent the entire day with the device on backward, and the punishment was to put it on and take it off ten times in a row.

"Not like that!" From behind, iron hands seized the ties and yanked them to strangulation level. "It's supposed to be snug!"

"Hey, that hurts!"

"Perfect," Radford confirmed. "If it's comfortable, it's on wrong. Ten more times, Archie."

Will smoldered as the mate strode away. It was humiliating! Why wouldn't Radford let him do this in the privacy of the crew cabin? He had to be out here in front of everybody — even

Lyssa. She wasn't saying anything, but he could feel her scorn.

She stood behind the wheel of the *Phoenix*, piloting the schooner through the waves. Captain Cascadden was at her side, beaming his approval.

Wouldn't you know it! Out of the six of them, his sister was turning into the star sailing pupil — while he was the sweat-hog in the back row, too stupid to figure out how to put on a life jacket.

Look at her, chatting with the captain like they're old friends. A bitter taunt began to form in his mind, something like: *Hey, Lyss, make sure you don't slip in any of that barf from yesterday!* But he didn't dare say it with Cascadden right there.

Besides, Lyssa wasn't letting the seasickness bother her at all. Lyssa, who had more reason to hate this trip than anybody, actually seemed to be liking it!

I should have been an only child.

The captain resumed his stance at the wheel, while Lyssa began examining various gauges and dials on the control console.

Yeah, right, thought Will. *Like she knows what she's looking at.*

He watched as his sister's features contracted into a frown. "Captain, I forget. What does it mean again when the barometer is falling so fast you can see it moving?"

The captain scanned the glassy sky to the west. The line of black clouds was as solid as a wall stretching clear across the horizon.

CHAPTER NINE
Saturday, July 15, 1750 hours

The news from the weather fax was all bad.

A tropical storm near the equator had suddenly turned their way. It was set to collide with a large mass of cooler air dipping down from the north.

Will was making deals even before the captain explained their situation. *If the storm misses us, I'll keep my room so clean you could eat off the floor!*

"So I'm afraid we've got a bit of a rough ride ahead of us tonight," the captain told them grimly.

"You mean last time *wasn't* a rough ride?" Charla said in dismay.

"My dear," the captain replied evenly, "last time was a lap around the duck pond compared with what the next few hours might bring us. But the *Phoenix* is a fine ship. We'll make it through if we keep our heads."

The first order of business was to take down the sails.

"I can't believe they're making us do this by hand!" complained J.J. as he and Luke hauled on the main halyard. "There's a storm coming, and we're doing work when we don't have to!"

"Hey!" Luke said sharply. "This is no time to get on the captain's nerves."

"But it's such a *snow job!*" He belted out the last two words so they would reach the mate on the ratlines. Radford glared down at them.

They heard the engine come to life. The *Phoenix* would face this gale under power.

The weather roared up quickly. At dusk, the rain started pelting down on them. The wind came with the dark — a blustery blow that had the crew hanging onto bulwarks and rigging as they made their way around the deck. Mr. Radford handed out life jackets and safety harnesses.

"Always keep your belt locked onto something that's attached to the boat," he ordered sternly. "When you move from place to place, hang on with two hands. Don't be embarrassed to crawl. Got it?"

The waves grew, slowly but steadily. At first, they weren't any bigger than the seas that had turned the *Phoenix* into a roller coaster ride a day before. But Luke could see they were more dangerous. Yesterday the swells had been like mountains, forcing the schooner to climb and descend, climb and descend from peak to peak. These were more like a series of oncoming cliffs, vertical walls of water. A ship can't climb a cliff. Instead, wave after wave broke over the bow, sending a constant knee-deep flood surging across the deck.

Ian's feet were swept out from under him — and down he went. Luke caught him and yanked him upright.

Luke wasn't sure whether or not to be alarmed. The storm was howling worse every minute, but the captain and mate were working calmly and efficiently in the battering wind and rain.

"This is bad, right?" he shouted to Mr. Radford. "Shouldn't we go below?"

"Don't panic, Archie!" ordered the mate. "Let's batten everything down first."

"No!" J.J. protested "We don't have to get blown around like this!"

Radford shot him a fierce look. "You gonna ask your famous daddy to pay off the storm and make it go away?"

"We can outrun it!" J.J. argued. "We've got more wind than we know what to do with! Just put up the sails and fly!"

Radford shook his head in disgust and rushed away.

J.J. threw up his arms. "What'd I say?"

He got a faceful of spray for his answer.

Great patches of foam blew in dense streaks. At one point, Luke looked over the gunwale and saw nothing but white water — not a speck of blue or green. Every minute or so, the *Phoenix* was lifted bodily and then flung contemptuously aside by a thirty-foot wave.

The deck lurched violently. Unlike yesterday's up and down, the tumbling of the sea was heavy and shocklike. Even athletic Charla couldn't keep her balance. She sat down on the cabin top and tried to slide along on her behind. Will crawled across the deck on all fours, unable to trust his own feet. A rush of sea washed over him, leaving him flopping and sputtering.

Lyssa was clamped onto the ratlines, her face green. "I'm gonna lose it!" she warned.

"That's so typical!" howled her brother, spitting salt water. "All day long you're Sinbad the Sailor, and now you can't hang on to your lunch!"

Radford turned to the cockpit. "We're secure, Skipper!"

Harnessed to the wheel stand, Captain Cascadden was barely visible through the rain, foam, and spray. Out of the chaos came his order. "All hands below!"

"You don't have to ask *me* twice!" exclaimed Will, sprint-crawling for the companionway to the main cabin.

Lyssa was hot on his heels, followed by Charla, high-stepping to keep her balance. Next came Luke, dragging Ian by the arm. At the last second, a huge wave broke over the bow, jolting the stern upward and pitching the two boys down the companionway.

Radford hooted with laughter. "You guys should join the circus — the flying Archie brothers!" His brow clouded as he did a head count. "Where's Richie Rich?"

Luke froze as J.J.'s words came back to him: *Just put up the sails and fly!* "That maniac," he muttered, clamboring up the companionway again.

"Hey!" barked the mate. "Get back here, Archie!"

At that moment, J.J. was clamped around the wrapped mainsail, hanging on with one hand and untying lines with the other.

When the furled sail was free, he stood up. Instantly, he was thrown to the deck. His father had once gotten him a bit part in a movie — an earthquake scene. There had been thirty special effects guys underneath them, pitching the floor every which way. It was *nothing* compared with the *Phoenix* right now! They had to get out of here! They could beat this storm no matter what Radford said! All they needed was some sail. . . .

Crouching low, he dashed astern through the rain and spray, steadying himself with an arm on the cabin top. He peered around the corner and set his eyes on the instrument panel behind the wheel. Six, maybe seven feet away. He'd be seen, but by then it would be too late — *if* he could keep from falling flat on his face!

Counting silently — one, two, *three!* — he launched himself past the captain and reached for the mechanism that raised the mainsail.

Luke hit him at hip height, diving like a linebacker. The two of them fell hard to the slick deck.

"What the — ?" The captain spun around to face them. "What are you doing here, crewmen? Get yourselves below!"

"You lunatic!" Luke rasped at J.J. "You'll get us all killed!"

"I know what I'm doing!" J.J. insisted frantically. He lunged for the panel, but Luke grabbed him once more.

"Archie!" Radford struggled onto the scene. The beam of his flashlight captured Luke and J.J. locked in a wrestling match.

"Break it up!" ordered Cascadden. He un-

SHIPWRECK

hooked his safety harness and stepped between the two combatants, separating them with a heave of his powerful arms.

The schooner lurched suddenly, and J.J. was tossed off his feet. The deck wash had him, was about to sweep him away. In a single motion, Captain Cascadden clamped his right hand onto J.J.'s wrist and reached back with the left, groping for something, anything, to hold on to. His fingers closed on the side of the instrument panel and gripped hard. His palm pressed against a small button.

The roar of the waves covered the mechanical *clunk* as the mainsail began to rise automatically.

Radford ran over, and he and the captain set J.J. back up on his feet.

"*Captain!*" Luke spotted the white canvas flapping wildly as it rose from its boom. "The *sail!*"

Captain and mate turned just as the fifty-knot wind filled the half-open mainsail with an overpowering force.

It was as if the whole world suddenly tilted ninety degrees. The sixty-foot boat was blown all the way over on its side, its masts barely out of the water. Radford grabbed the mainsheet, which now extended over his head like monkey bars. The captain hung on to J.J. and the instrument panel.

The next thing Luke knew, he was moving, falling parallel to the deck. Only the gunwale — eighteen inches of wood — stood between him and a violent ocean.

Wham! He bounced off like a Ping-Pong ball, snatching wildly for the lifeline. He felt the wire in his hands and held on, his feet dragging in the water.

"Archie!" Radford called. "Lock your harness on the lifeline!"

"I can't!" he tried to answer, but a torrent of sea and spray found his throat. He came up choking.

Waves crashed over the twin masts. The automatic halyard winch ground to a halt.

The captain secured J.J.'s safety belt around the wheel stand. Then he hit the button to lower the mainsail.

Nothing happened.

"No power to the winch!" howled Radford. "I'll have to lower it manually!"

Like Tarzan moving from vine to vine, the mate grabbed the halyard and swung over. He hung there, trying to use his full weight to pull the sail down. "Too much blow, skipper!" he called. "I can't budge it!"

"Take the helm, crewman!" the captain ordered J.J. He heaved himself up on the side of the cabin top to make his way over to the mate.

Clinging to the wire at the starboard gunwale, Luke was the first to see the great wave. It was enormous — a forty-footer — curling over the high side of the *Phoenix* like a giant hand about to crush the small ship.

He shouted, "Captain — !"

And then the monster broke. To Luke it seemed like Niagara Falls raging down the upturned deck toward him.

Crack!

The mainmast snapped like a toothpick under the weight of the thundering sea. An avalanche of rope and canvas pelted down. As if in slow motion, the broken peak of the mast toppled over, striking Captain Cascadden across the shoulders.

Fierce lightning backlit a terrifying scene. Luke watched in horror as the captain was pitched from the deck into the foaming ocean.

"Man overboard!" he tried to shout.

But the force of the wave drove the gunwale of the *Phoenix* — and Luke with it — deep beneath the rampaging sea.

CHAPTER TEN
Saturday, July 15, 2015 hours

Underwater.

It was a strangely quiet and peaceful place. Luke was in a trance, experiencing a few seconds in a slow, almost lazy time warp of crystal-clear thought. He was going to drown — he was sure of that. The *Phoenix* was sinking, taking everybody with it. Even if he could make it back to the surface, then what? A lone swimmer — even one with a life jacket — had no chance against thirty-foot waves.

It was almost funny. Luke Haggerty had avoided Williston. Instead he had chosen — a *death sentence.*

The gunwale sprang back out of the sea as the *Phoenix* righted herself with heart-stopping suddenness. Luke lost his grip on the lifeline and sailed through the rain and spray. Flying again . . .

The pitching deck swung up to meet him. There was a painful thud, and he saw stars. He looked around. He was right in front of the cockpit. There, a terrified J.J. clung to the wheel, wrapped in rigging and torn canvas.

SHIPWRECK

"The captain — !" Luke gasped, choking and spitting.

J.J. was sobbing out of control. "I'm sorry! I'm sorry! I'm sorry! — "

"*Did you find the captain?!*"

J.J. shook his head. "He told me to hang on to the wheel!"

"You picked a heck of a time to start following orders!"

Mr. Radford waited for a break in the wave action to roll like a landing parachutist to the starboard deck. He clamped his harness onto a bulwark and began hurling life preservers into the water.

"Skipper! *Skipper!*" He panned the waves with his flashlight.

"The mast hit him!" Luke shouted, tethering his belt to the base of the instrument panel. "He could be unconscious!"

The mate leaped for the cockpit, shoving J.J. aside with a football straight-arm that left the boy swinging like a pendulum in his harness. Radford grabbed the throttle and thrust it forward. "We're circling back!"

With a cough and a sputter, the engine died. Cursing, the mate tried to restart it. It turned over but wouldn't catch. Then it stopped turning over. "Check the engine room, Archie!"

"We can't unhook our belts!" Luke protested.

"Right below you!"

Luke knelt down and threw open the hatch. There was the engine, half submerged in three feet of water. He turned to the mate, but his mouth couldn't form words. Fear had frozen his jaw.

"Well?" Radford prompted angrily.

J.J. supplied the answer in the form of a question. "If we're flooded here, does that mean the whole boat's flooded?"

Charla's upper body emerged from the main cabin. "We've got water down here!" she cried.

"How much?" called the mate.

"A couple of feet at least!"

"Son of a — " The mate switched on the electric bilge pump. It was as dead as the engine.

"Get on the manual pumps!" he roared.

"What about the captain?" Luke insisted.

"We're looking for him!"

J.J. pointed frantically astern. "But he's back there somewhere!"

"We can't get back there without engine power!" Radford snarled. "*He* has to find *us*! Get all hands on deck to man the pumps!"

Luke saw Captain Cascadden in every wave, heard a call for help in every gust of wind. His eyes searched the backwash of each breaker that rocked the deck, half-expecting the ocean to return the old sailor to his ship.

J.J. never stopped yelling, "Captain! *Captain!*" He got no answer.

The feeling of hope on the schooner was so strong that Luke could almost reach out and touch it, could taste it in the salt spray. But it was only a feeling, trumped by the reality: pumping — hard work, simple, repeating, exhausting. No one dared unhook the safety harness for fear of being pitched overboard as the *Phoenix* was brutalized by the killer storm.

It was hours and it felt like years before the wind began to subside. The rain kept coming, but it weakened — a soaking shower rather than a driving attack. The terrible lightning ceased. Finally, the waves rounded off.

When Mr. Radford ordered them all to bed, nobody asked about the captain.

They already knew.

CHAPTER ELEVEN
Sunday, July 16, 0825 hours

Luke awoke with blond hair in his face. He tried to sit up and couldn't budge an inch.

"Man overboard . . . man overboard . . ." murmured a voice beside him, very close.

J.J.

Luke started to complain and then remembered. The captain . . .

He shut his eyes tightly and shook his head, but the awful image wouldn't go away — the six-foot-five Cascadden, disappearing into the foam.

When Radford had finally ordered them to bed, the lower bunks were underwater. They were sharing the uppers, packed like sardines, two to a berth, strapped in with lee canvases.

Luke leaned over to unfasten the hook, elbowing J.J. awake in the process.

"I had a nightmare," J.J. mumbled.

"No, you didn't," Luke told him soberly.

Will peered out from the bunk he shared with Ian. "Is it just me, or is the water getting higher?"

J.J. jumped down with a splash. "Feel that? Calm. And look." He pointed outside. "Sun's back."

SHIPWRECK

The four sloshed out of bed and climbed up the companionway. On deck, crusted sea salt crunched under their feet. In the light of day, the *Phoenix* was a floating plate of spaghetti — rope and rigging lay tangled everywhere. The mainmast looked like giant hands had snapped it in two. Equipment, most of it smashed, was deposited in clumps all over the deck. The radio antenna was gone, and the bowsprit was cracked and off-center. The ship's dinghy, which was usually stowed upside down in the rigging, was now pointed straight up, as if it were a rocket about to be launched at the moon.

Ian summed up everybody's feelings when he said, "Wow."

Lyssa and Charla worked one of the pumps, trying to clear the water out of the engine room. Mr. Radford manned the other, which was draining the main cabin and galley.

All activity ceased when they saw the boys on deck.

J.J. spoke first. "Shouldn't we still try looking for the captain?"

Radford stood up. If looks could kill, J.J. would have been fried to a crisp. "To look for the captain, you don't use a boat; you use a submarine."

"Hey!" Luke said angrily. "You're talking about a real guy who died. It's not a joke."

"No, it's not," the mate agreed unpleasantly. "Someday I want to sit down with you and your friend Richie Rich and find out why you needed to play WWF in a full gale. You damn near got us all killed. And you *did* get one of us killed."

Dan Rapaport's words at the Guam airport echoed in J.J.'s ears: *You're going to kill somebody one of these days. . . .*

"Well, don't blame me!" Luke exclaimed hotly. "I was trying to keep this maniac from raising the sails just to show you he knew how!"

"Not true," said J.J. in a hollow tone. "I thought I could help — "

"Next time," snarled Radford, "help somebody else."

Lyssa stepped forward. "Let's forget about who did what and concentrate on how we're going to get out of this."

Calmly, the mate went over their situation. According to the GPS, they were four hundred eighty miles east-northeast of Guam. Nearest landfall: Guam. No SOS had been sent, and the radio was out. Even if the radio could be fixed, the call couldn't travel much more than fifteen or twenty miles without an antenna. Their only chance of being spotted depended on the schooner's Emergency Position Indicating Radiobeacon — EPIRB. This was unlikely to reach other ships but might be detected by passing airplanes.

"How many air routes fly over this part of the Pacific?" asked Luke.

"None," Radford replied.

The engine was dead and full of seawater, which pretty much guaranteed that it would never work again. The mainsail was gone, and the staysail and jibs couldn't be used because of the damage to the bowsprit. That left just the foresail. It was fine — if they could ever get past the thousands of pounds of tangled ropes and fallen rigging.

The drinking-water tanks were okay. But there was no electricity and no refrigeration. The food stores and medical supplies were at least partly damaged by salt water.

Worst of all, the *Phoenix* wasn't expected in for three weeks. That meant no one was looking for them.

"Are we going to *die?*" asked Will in a small voice.

"I won't lie to you," said Radford. "We're in big, big trouble. To get through this we're going to have to work twenty-hour days, ration our supplies, and — " he glared at Luke and J.J. " — no more crazy stunts! We've lost a man already, and we're all going to have to live with that — *if* we live."

*   *   *

According to the mate, there were three main jobs that needed to be done to ensure their survival.

1. Pumping. "Pump like your life depends on it . . . because it does."

2. Clearing the foresail. "If we go anywhere, that's how we'll get there."

3. Lightening the ship. "If we can't eat it, wear it, or sail it, we pitch it."

That included luggage, books, all pots, pans, and dishes except the bare minimum, and the waterlogged mattresses off the lower bunks. The drawers from the built-in dressers went over the side next, along with any cartons of spoiled food from the galley.

"Are you sure we should be doing this?" Charla asked nervously. She watched a load of instant mashed potatoes swell up like a swamp creature before sinking out of sight. "It can't be good for the environment to just throw garbage in the ocean."

"Are you kidding?" Lyssa managed to manufacture a smile as she pumped. "These fish never had it so good. They're probably going to ask us for gravy."

Mr. Radford clung to the mainmast, chopping at the splintered wood with an ax. Will and Ian worked at the tangle of rigging with hacksaws. It took until noon, but all hands paused to watch the top of the mast and hundreds of pounds of ropes and shredded canvas slide over the side and disappear under the waves. It brought up a halfhearted cheer. Even Mr. Radford added a grunt of approval.

Lunch was the *Phoenix*'s entire store of frozen hot dogs, which were thawing out since there was no electricity for the freezer.

Charla made a face. "Any vegetables?"

The mate pulled out a huge tub of chocolate ice cream and tossed it to her.

"I can't eat this!" she exclaimed.

"Wait a few hours," grunted Radford. "You can drink it."

She bit her lip. Without the captain around, that terrible man was becoming meaner and more obnoxious. She felt instantly guilty. Was that all the captain meant to her — an authority figure to keep Radford in line? How selfish was that?

While the crew was eating, the mate let himself over the side and down the swim ladder to check the waterline on the hull. When he came back, his face was gray.

"Not enough!" he panted. "We've got to dump more gear!"

"There's nothing left to dump," J.J. protested.

Radford looked at him sourly. "Don't tempt me, Richie Rich."

They removed the boom of the mainsail and slid it into the water. The galley's refrigerator and the backup generator — both ruined — were next.

Then the mate's attention fell on the *Phoenix*'s three anchors. One by one, they were cut loose and dropped into the sea.

Luke was worried. "What if we need one of those to — you know — anchor?"

"If we get that close to land, Archie," Radford promised, "I'll jump in and hold the boat personally."

"Hey, what's the big idea?" demanded J.J. from the open cargo hatch. He stepped onto the deck, dragging a large bright yellow suitcase. "I had to leave my Jet Ski in Hawaii! But someone's allowed to bring the world's biggest piece of luggage on board!" He fiddled with the catch. "Whose is this?"

Radford's eyes bulged. "No!"

Pow!

With a hiss of compressed gas, the "suitcase" burst open, shooting out to ten times its original size. J.J. was knocked back into the flooded cargo hold, where he landed with a mammoth splash. The thing kept on growing, unfolding at the corners like a flower. By the time J.J.'s head poked out of the hold, an eight-foot rubber life raft sat on deck, complete with sun canopy, seating for ten, signal flares, first aid kit, and provisions.

The roar that came from Radford was barely human. "Why is it always you, Richie Rich?"

J.J. was soaked and sulky. "You should have told me there was a boat in there."

"The label said CONTENTS: ONE LIFEBOAT. What did you want? A singing telegram?"

"We'll just fold it up again," J.J. said defensively. "What's the big deal?"

"The big deal is you *can't* fold it up again!" the mate howled. "It has to go back to the factory to be recharged!"

"Well, that's stupid."

"Yes, it is! And it's even stupider to waste our precious space tying this thing down so it doesn't blow out to sea with the next puff of breeze!"

Will spent the day cringing as he waited for the mate's furious criticism to fall on him. Everyone was getting yelled at — even little Miss Perfect, Lyssa. When she delivered the news that their EPIRB had conked out, Radford hollered at her like she had personally smashed it with a hammer. Maybe Captain Cascadden had thought Lyssa could do no wrong. But Radford was an equal-opportunity offender.

It was tough to be captain's pet when the captain wasn't around anymore.

Instantly, Will felt terrible for his thoughts. A man was dead and gone, and he was almost celebrating the fact that it made things harder for Lyssa.

If, by some miracle, the captain turns out to be okay, I'll take out the garbage; I'll give to charity if I ever get any money; I'll be a better person, I swear!

The problem with the EPIRB turned out to be a fixable one. J.J.'s inflatable lifeboat had its own beacon, which was moved to the navigation room and switched on.

"You're welcome," J.J. gloated. "Opening that raft seems like a pretty smart move now, huh?"

It was the kind of comment that would have guaranteed a screaming broadside from the old Radford. But the mate gave no sign that he'd even heard. Something had changed about him — almost as if there had been an audible click.

Later, when Radford went over the side to recheck the waterline of the boat, Luke was waiting for him at the swim ladder. "How are we doing? Do we need to get rid of more stuff?"

Radford grunted and wouldn't answer.

At four o'clock, when he went to assess the water in the hull, Lyssa went with him to hold the flashlight.

"It looks worse than ever," she said in concern. "Are you sure all that pumping is doing any good?"

The mate remained sullen and silent.

"I liked him better when he was yelling at us," was Will's opinion. "You know where you stand with a guy who hates you. But one who ignores you — that's scary."

"I miss the captain," Ian said simply.

Long faces nodded all around.

At dinner, the mate wouldn't even eat with them. He took a tin of cold beans and sat atop the main cabin, staring into the sunset and shoveling with a plastic spoon.

It was a moonless night — impossible to tell the *Phoenix* from the vast ocean around her. Luke couldn't see his own sneakers without a flashlight, and the crew walked carefully despite the calm waters.

It had taken all day, but the foresail had finally emerged from the mountain of tangled ropes and rigging.

"I think it's ready," Luke called to Mr. Radford.

The mate was still atop the main cabin — flat

on his back now, staring up at the stars.

"We're ready to raise the foresail," Luke repeated, louder this time.

No answer.

Ian tried his luck. "Excuse me," he ventured. "Uh — Mr. Rat-face?"

A collective gasp went up on deck. J.J. stopped pumping and laughed out loud.

The mate sat up suddenly. "What? What did you call me?"

"Mr. — " Ian caught a desperate look from Luke and realized his mistake. The younger boy went pale.

"Foresail's ready," Luke put in quickly. "Want us to raise it?"

Radford jumped down from the cabin top. Even in the pitch-black, they could see his burning eyes glaring at them. But when he finally spoke, his tone was light and easygoing.

"Tomorrow's another day," he said. "Why don't you kids get some sleep? I'll look after things up here."

"What about pumping?" asked Lyssa.

"You can't save your life if you kill yourself doing it," the mate told her. He paused. "You did a lot of good work today — in a tough situation. I'm — " His face twisted. "I'm proud of you."

Will held it in until the four boys were splashing around the cabin. "Mr. Rat-face!" he guffawed at Ian. "Man, I was expecting him to go berserk and throw you overboard!"

"I thought it was his name," Ian said honestly.

"Nobody's name is Rat-face!" Luke exclaimed, hoisting himself onto the upper berth and drying his wet feet with a towel. "Not even in TV land!"

Ian flushed. "You know how sometimes you hear a word, but you don't think about what it really means? It's just *sounds* to you."

Luke patted him on the shoulder. "We forgive you, kid. He needed to hear it, anyway."

"Well, he didn't get mad," the younger boy added. "In fact, I thought he was pretty nice about it."

"Yeah, right," snickered J.J. "Radford — nice. That's a good one."

CHAPTER TWELVE
Monday, July 17, 0645 hours

"Will! Wake up!"

Will rolled over and cast a baleful eye at his sister. "Beat it, Lyss. You're not supposed to be in here."

"Come on!" She dragged him out of the narrow bunk. His elbow smacked Ian in the back of the head as he splashed to the deck. The water was now well over his knees, halfway to his waist.

"Ow!" The younger boy sat up. "What's going on?"

"Yeah!" stormed Will. "This better be good, Lyssa!"

"Radford's gone."

"Gone?" scoffed J.J. "Where could he go? Out for a stroll?"

"He just — disappeared," she said. "Maybe he fell off the boat."

"I couldn't get that lucky," grumbled Luke. "Besides, Rat-face is a career sailor. He'd never go overboard, not in calm seas like this."

Up on deck they found Charla waiting for them.

SHIPWRECK

"Notice anything missing?" she asked.

"You mean besides one psychopath?" J.J. retorted.

She pointed to the rigging around the foresail. There hung the inflatable lifeboat, exactly where they had stowed it the day before. But the *Phoenix*'s twelve-foot wooden dinghy was gone. "He must have sailed off in the middle of the night. Took the GPS too. And most of our food."

"He *left* us?" Ian was wide-eyed. "All alone?"

"Impossible," Will insisted. "Nobody's that rotten. Not even Radford."

"It doesn't make sense," said Luke. "Why would he set out in a wooden bathtub? Surely it's better to stay on a sixty-foot boat."

"It's not exactly in mint condition," Lyssa put in. "The mast's busted, the bowsprit's useless — "

"Not to mention the cabins are full of water — " added Charla.

It took a few seconds for the truth to seep down.

"We're sinking!" cried Will. "That's why Radford split! Water's coming in faster than we can pump it out! And he knew!"

Shocked silence followed. All six waited for someone to speak out, to say, "Of course not!

That's not what's happening at all. *Here's* the real story — "

But the facts were undeniable. They had pumped all day to lower the water level, and in the morning it was high again — higher even. The schooner was leaking — *sinking* — and they were on their own.

Heart pounding, Luke thought back to the moment yesterday when the mate had gone from his usual loudmouthed, bullying self to quiet, sullen, and withdrawn. In that instant, Rat-face must have made up his mind to desert them. He might as well have signed their death warrants. What chance did six inexperienced kids have on a sinking boat?

The unfairness of it suddenly seemed so weighty that it threatened to crush him. He was only here because he'd trusted a false friend with his locker combination. Never in Luke's wildest nightmares had he imagined it would cost him his life.

"That scumball," he said finally.

"Oh, *no*," breathed Lyssa.

Charla sat down on the deck, her head in her hands.

"It's all my fault!" moaned Ian. "I messed up his name. I got him mad at us!"

SHIPWRECK

"Hey!" Luke grabbed him by the shoulder. "You don't leave people to die because somebody made fun of you. God, to do something like this, you've got to be *evil!*"

"So what do we do now?" asked Will in a daze. "We just *sink*, and that's it?"

"That's what Radford must think," Luke said seriously. "If we make it to some port and tell the story of how he deserted us, he's in big trouble. In his mind, we're already fish food."

"He's right," gasped Will, fighting back tears.

"How do *you* know?" Lyssa snapped angrily.

"He's a sailor!" he yelled. "He knows a sinking boat when he sees one, idiot!"

"Not now," commanded Luke. "We have to think. There must be something we can do."

"We can pump," Charla ventured.

"Radford knew that," Lyssa pointed out, "and he still split."

"But it'll buy us time," Luke argued. "Every gallon we pump out must mean a few more minutes before we sink. Now, what else have we got?"

"The foresail," said Ian. "We never raised it, but it's ready."

"And the engine," Lyssa added thoughtfully. "I could be wrong, but it's just wet."

"Wet?" cried her brother. "It's underwater!"

"We pump out the engine room, take the motor apart, dry it out" — her eyes gleamed " — maybe I can put it back together again."

"This isn't your science fair project!" Will exploded. "It's real life!"

"Well, have you got a better idea?" she shot back.

J.J. shook his head. "Could I just say something?" One by one, he looked them in the eye. "No offense, but I've never seen such a bunch of total *saps* in my life!"

"Oh, no offense taken," Luke said unkindly.

"Seriously," J.J. persisted. "I mean, don't you think all this is a little too convenient?"

Luke looked daggers at him. "No, I think it's pretty *inconvenient* that Rat-face left us for dead in the middle of the Pacific Ocean. And when the boat sinks, that'll be even less convenient!"

"The boat's not sinking," scoffed J.J. "And Radford didn't leave us either."

Will was confused. "Then where is he?"

The actor's son shrugged. "On another boat just out of sight, watching us through binoculars. And you know who's with him? The captain."

"You're sick!" stormed Luke. "The captain's dead. I saw him go over the side, and so did you!"

J.J. chuckled. "The special effects guys who

work on my dad's movies — they can make anything seem like anything. The captain's 'death,' the sinking boat, Radford's disappearance — they faked all that."

"But why?" Charla asked in a small voice.

"To see how we'll react under pressure," J.J. explained. "That's CNC's whole gig! Cooperation. Teamwork. They're probably watching us right now, making notes on what we say and do. I'll bet they've got hidden cameras and microphones all over this boat."

"You know what?" said Luke. "You're crazy."

"I'm the only sane one here," J.J. replied coolly.

"I've got news for you," Luke told him. "You're not the center of the universe. Nobody's watching you through hidden cameras. If this boat sinks, you're going to drown along with the rest of us, because the ocean doesn't care who your daddy is!"

"That's your opinion," J.J. said smugly. "If you guys want to break your backs on those pumps, then be my guest. *I'm* on vacation. If anybody needs me, I'll be working on my tan."

And before their shocked eyes, J.J. Lane spread a towel across the cabin top, flaked out on it, and surrendered his body to the sun's rays.

CHAPTER THIRTEEN
Monday, July 17, 1440 hours

It was fairly easy to raise the foresail and get the *Phoenix* moving again. But as to whether or not it was in the right direction — that was anybody's guess. Radford had given their last position as east-northeast of Guam. Even though they had drifted a lot since that reading, they were following the compass west-southwest. It seemed the only course.

"I don't know," Luke said uneasily. "We're probably wasting our time. We could be getting even more lost than before."

"In a crisis," lectured Ian, "it's always best to keep busy to prevent the onset of panic."

Luke stared at the boy who spoke so seldom that they often had to remind themselves he was aboard. "Since when did you become ship's counselor?"

Ian flushed. "I saw it on a documentary once."

Luke sighed. "Ian, did anyone ever tell you that you watch too much TV?"

"My parents." Ian nodded sadly. "Right before they put me on this trip."

SHIPWRECK

Luke sent Ian below to the navigation room to see if he could find any maps — *charts*, the captain had always called them. In open ocean there were no landmarks. But it might be helpful to know the course the *Phoenix* had been following before disaster struck.

He watched the younger boy's careful footsteps. The schooner's deck now sloped dangerously down toward the bow. This was because both pumps were working in the engine room near the stern. For the time being, anyway, they were letting the forward compartments fill up with water. It was a big risk, no question about it. If the *Phoenix* got too far out of balance, Luke reflected, it could take a diagonal dive just like the *Titanic*.

But tough times called for tough choices. They needed the engine, and Lyssa couldn't fix it if the thing was underwater.

Luke looked up, squinting in the sunlight. He could barely make out Charla perched atop the foremast. She was scanning the horizon for signs of other ships, ready to fire off distress flares if she spotted anything. The job had fallen to her mostly because she was the only one with the guts to climb up the ratlines — her and J.J. But Luke doubted J.J., the daredevil, would be interested unless there was a reasonable chance of killing himself. And besides, the actor's son was boycotting the effort to be rescued, still convinced that their current peril was all part of CNC's plan.

Lyssa had already started taking apart the motor, even though the engine room was still under two feet of water. She was working by snorkel mask. Every few minutes she would surface like a submarine, and another wet part would hit the drying towel with a dull clink.

Will's official job was pumper, but he doubled as a nervous nag. "You remember where that piece goes, right?" he kibitzed down the open engine hatch. "You'll know how to put it back together?"

"No," she said sarcastically. "I'm busting it up just to get you killed."

Will couldn't decide what made him more uneasy — their current danger, or the fact that Lyssa was emerging as the big hero.

Ian came running up the companionway, waving a thick folder with the CNC logo on the cover.

"You found the maps?" Luke asked.

Ian shook his head. "Files."

"Files?" Luke repeated.

"On us."

Luke gave Ian the wheel and fished through his own folder. Now that he thought about it, of course Charting a New Course would need information on its charges. Still, it was eerie to see his whole life between the covers — almost like the FBI had been keeping tabs on him. But this stuff must have come from his parents. There were school pictures and report cards; medical records — it said he'd been allergic to milk as a baby. Was that true? No one had ever mentioned anything to him.

All the court documents were in there, along with the arrest report and his suspension papers from school. And — what was this?

Luke recognized his mother's handwriting on the letter:

. . . Luke is a good boy, but lately he's been running with a tough crowd, including a boy named Reese, who has had trouble with the law before. We want to believe him when he says that the gun wasn't his, but we don't want to be naive either — not where Luke's future is concerned. We can't take the chance that this Reese has gotten him involved with a gang. We think it might be a good idea to get him away from here for a while. Therefore, we're accepting the court's proposal to send him to you. . . .

Luke put the letter down, blinking hard. "They *said* they believed me."

By this time, all pumping work had stopped for the crew members to dig into their files. Lyssa emerged from the engine room and Charla abandoned her lookout post to join them. Even J.J. interrupted his tanning to flip quickly through his folder.

He was unimpressed. "Big deal. So I'm a flake. What else is new?" He peered over Ian's shoulder. "Couch potato. No friends. What a surprise."

"Lay off," Luke warned.

But J.J. had already moved on to Will and Lyssa. "Whoa, what are you guys, hit men? There isn't this much violence in the James Bond movies!"

Will flushed. "I don't know how it happens. One minute we're just arguing — "

Lyssa cut him off. "Shut up, Will! We don't have to explain anything. Mind your own business, rich boy."

J.J. shrugged. "I don't see any of you guys in the poorhouse. CNC doesn't come cheap, you know."

"You find the money," Luke put in grimly, "when your two choices are either here or jail."

SHIPWRECK

"Or you borrow it," Charla added bitterly. "Not all of us live in Beverly Hills."

"Yeah, what's *your* story?" asked J.J., snatching the folder from her hands.

She reacted like a wildcat. "Give that back!"

J.J. held the file up out of her reach and kept on reading over his head.

Charla leaped like a basketball player, grabbed the papers from his hand, and fixed him with a withering glare. "Moron," she muttered.

He looked bewildered. "What'd I do?"

"That's private!" she raged.

"You know what it says? That you're world-class at, like, fifteen sports. What a deep, dark secret! My own father sends me halfway around the world just so he won't have to look at me, but you don't want anyone to find out you're a star!"

"You didn't get to the part where it says what a head case I am," she mumbled.

"We're all head cases," J.J. told her. "This is a trip for head cases. That's why we're here."

Lyssa pushed her snorkel mask back down over her face. "Well, this was fun — " She stepped into the engine hatch.

J.J. regarded the pile of folders. "What are we going to do with these?"

Luke glared at him. "You really want to hear my suggestion?"

J.J. picked up the files and walked to the gunwale. With the exaggerated windup of a major league pitcher, he flung them into the sea.

"How's the environment now?" he asked Charla.

"It'll live," she replied, tight-lipped.

"Well, let's get back to work," said J.J.

Luke raised an eyebrow. "Look who's admitting that we might be in trouble."

"I'm bored, that's all," J.J. insisted. "Gotta have something to do till the cavalry arrives. Which pump is mine?"

CHAPTER FOURTEEN
Monday, July 17, 1640 hours

As the day wore on, Luke watched the bow of the *Phoenix* sink lower and lower into the sea. At least a dozen times he was tempted to send the pumpers forward to try to even out the schooner's balance.

No. If they had a chance, it was with the motor. They had to pump out the engine room first.

It was an agonizing decision. If they took a nosedive to the bottom, it would be all his fault.

Even in a glassy calm, sleepy waves broke over the gunwale. The water puddled for only a moment before rolling down a deck that was sloped like a parking ramp. If another storm blew through, the *Phoenix* wouldn't last five minutes.

In the crew cabins, even the upper bunks were swamped now. Where the crew members were supposed to sleep was anybody's guess. Probably they just wouldn't sleep anymore. Luke thought back to the night before, crammed next to J.J. in the narrow berth. That misery might go down as his final night of sleep ever. The thought coaxed a nervous chuckle from him, but beneath

ISLAND

the surface lingered a feeling so awful he didn't dare dwell on it.

By five o'clock the entire engine was spread across two beach towels in the stern.

Will surveyed the scene with a frown. "I hope you can look at this stuff and see a motor, because all I see is a huge pile of junk."

Lyssa looked preoccupied. "I've got it straight in my mind. Don't bug me."

It took another hour to get the last few inches of thick murky slime off the floor of the engine room. Then Lyssa eased herself down the hatch to start the long task of reassembly. The pumpers rushed forward to work on the crew cabins and the fo'c'sle — the area belowdecks directly under the bow. They were exhausted, but there was no time for a break. As Luke put it, their next break could be spent on the ocean floor.

The sun was setting when Will stepped into the cockpit and joined Luke at the wheel. He checked their direction — still west-southwest. "How do we know that's right?" he asked uneasily. "Maybe the compass is broken like everything else on this tub."

Luke shrugged. "You can't be off-course when you don't know where you're going in the first place." He regarded the foresail. "Wind's picking up. We should probably let out the sheet a little."

Will groaned. "If you're turning into a real sailor, I'm going to have to start treating you like Radford."

Luke shot Will a look. "Don't mention that name, not even as a joke."

Will shook his head. "How could anybody do what he did? I mean, we're talking about *dying* here! Are we so worthless to him?"

Luke looked at him sharply. "We're not worthless; Rat-face is worthless. If there's any justice in this world, he'll get his."

"Unless — " Will frowned. "You don't think J.J. could be right? That all this is part of the CNC thing?"

"It's pretty crazy," said Luke. "They'd have to trash their own boat, wash the captain into the sea on purpose. Anything's possible, I guess. I'd love to believe that the captain's okay."

"Me too," Will agreed fervently. "That's probably what's in J.J.'s head. He feels responsible."

"He *is* responsible," Luke said flatly. "He was born with a dream life. He gets whatever he wants whenever he wants it. And he's still the biggest screwup I've ever met."

Lyssa heaved herself through the engine room

hatch, dusting ineffectually at the caked muck on her knees.

Will looked at his sister anxiously but couldn't read her expression. "Tell me it's good news."

"It's back together," she replied. "That's all I know for sure."

"The captain said never to start the engine without the blower," Luke reminded her.

"The blower's electric," Lyssa explained. "If we run it before the engine's on, we could drain the battery charge — "

"English, Lyss," Will interrupted impatiently.

"We'll have to improvise." She picked up the grease-spattered beach towels that had been used to dry off the engine parts and tossed one to Luke and one to Will. "When I give the word, you guys stand over the hatch and fan like crazy."

Luke was amazed. "And that's safe?"

"She knows this stuff," Will said fervently. "She got an A on that science project."

Lyssa replaced Luke at the wheel and waited for the two boys to establish themselves above the hatch. "Okay — now!"

Like palace guards fanning the sultan, Luke and Will began waving their towels up and down, ventilating the engine room. Lyssa hit the starter button. The motor turned over, choked once, and died.

Will cursed and threw his towel to the deck.

"Don't stop!" she ordered briskly.

They resumed fanning and she tried again. This time the engine *put-putted* itself to life.

"All right, Lyss!" shouted Will.

His sister looked at him sharply but found no sarcasm in his praise.

Cheering and applause came from the pumpers above the crew cabins. Charla flashed them thumbs-up from her spot atop the foremast.

"Okay," exclaimed Luke, "put 'er in gear!"

Lyssa pushed forward on the throttle. The motor coughed and sputtered out.

"Aw, man!" moaned Will.

So the whole process began again. Luke and Will fanned while Lyssa tried to nurse the starter along.

"It's not easy, you know!" Will protested as the motor roared to life only to die with a wheeze and a hiccup of machinery. "It's murder on your shoulders!"

"You're such a crab," Lyssa sneered.

Luke rolled his eyes. What was with these two? They were on a sinking boat; this could be their last conversation. Why did it have to be fighting words?

As they continued to work and bicker, Luke noticed in alarm that the roar of the motor was becoming less and less frequent. After a few more minutes, the engine wouldn't even turn over.

Will was worried too. "Aw, Lyss, I knew you'd bust it!"

"Probably just flooded the carburetor," said Lyssa, grabbing the toolbox. "I can smell the gas." Once again, she lowered herself into the engine hatch.

"What's the problem?" Charla called.

Luke could only shrug. "You should come down. It's getting dark."

"Give me another half hour," came the reply. "I can still see a little."

After a few minutes, Lyssa emerged, reeking of fuel. "I think I've got it this time." She climbed into the cockpit and reached for the starter.

Luke and Will resumed fanning.

"My arm's falling off!" Will complained. He only let go for a second to rest his aching shoulder. But at that moment, a gust of wind snatched the greasy terry cloth from his other hand. The towel spread open like a full sail and floated slowly down over the engine hatch.

"Hey, wait — " Will began.

But Lyssa's oil-stained finger was already pressing the button.

The spark from the starter ignited the trapped fumes in the engine room. It made a *phoom*, like the lighting of a propane barbecue, only a lot louder. This was followed by a split-second pause as the fire shot up the fuel lines to the *Phoenix*'s ninety-gallon gas tanks.

"Get down!" howled Lyssa, hurling herself to the deck of the cockpit.

A mammoth explosion rocked the schooner, and for a moment, dusk was bright as day. Suddenly, the main cabin and galley were gone, replaced by a pillar of flame. The force of the blast threw Luke, Will, and Lyssa out over the transom, clear into the sea. Luke tasted salt water for a moment and then resurfaced into a burning hailstorm. Bits of cabin, deck, and galley — all on fire — pelted down on him, forcing him to dive. The blazing cookstove of the *Phoenix* hit the waves right where he had been a split second before.

On the foredeck, the shock wave knocked J.J. and Ian off their feet. When they recovered, they found themselves facing a wall of fire that engulfed two-thirds of the boat.

"The extinguisher!" cried Ian, reaching down the companionway and yanking the small tank from its mounting on the bulkhead. He pulled the pin and sprayed foam at the blaze. J.J. picked up a bucket and began bailing water from the cabins and sloshing it into the firestorm. The heat was unbearable, and they stumbled on the ruined deck, which was a tangle of twisted planks and splinters.

"It's no use!" bawled J.J. "We might as well be throwing Dixie cups of Kool-Aid!"

The blast had knocked Charla out of her post atop the foremast, landing her upside down in the ratlines. It took every ounce of her gymnastics training to right herself again. Through the waves of heat and smoke that billowed over her, she spotted J.J. and Ian. But when she looked aft, she saw only the boiling orange of the blaze.

"Where are the others?" she called down.

"In the stern!" shouted Ian.

"There *is* no stern! It's all fire back there!"

With a terrible creaking sound, the flaming stump of the mainmast toppled over in a shower of sparks. It crushed the cabin top, cutting the younger boy off from J.J.

"*Ian!*" J.J. cried.

Ian jumped back, stumbling on an upended deck board. The extinguisher dropped from his hands, rolled into the fire, and exploded in a *whoosh* of compressed gas.

The blazing mainmast ignited the foresail. J.J. sloshed water onto the smoldering sail, but flames quickly licked up the canvas, forcing Charla back atop the mast. The fire soon spread to the sheets and rigging.

"Ian, can you hear me?" called J.J.

"Get out of there!" came Ian's voice from the inferno.

J.J. spun around. "To *where?!*"

There were only two choices: Either stay on the burning boat or take his chances in the vast, inhospitable, and terrifying sea.

CHAPTER FIFTEEN
Monday, July 17, 1825 hours

Luke paddled like a four-year-old at his first swimming test. Just keeping his upper lip above water seemed almost impossible. This was crazy! He had a bronze badge from the Red Cross — why was he so helpless?

Panic and shock, he thought. And fear. He was trembling all over.

Stay close to the boat. That was the first rule for a man overboard. But a widening pool of burning gasoline was spreading around the *Phoenix,* making it look like the waves themselves were on fire. Luke found himself drifting farther and farther from the ship. If he got separated from the others, only the fish would find him.

"Luke!" It was a faint call from the gloom.

Will. The voice seemed to be coming from miles away, although Luke was sure Will couldn't be very far. "Will, are you okay?" he shouted.

No answer.

Luke looked around, fighting hysteria. The sun was down. Detail disappeared against the incandescent orange of the fire. He saw nothing. Except —

SHIPWRECK

There it was. A flash of color a few yards away. He made for it, splashing wildly.

In the pool at the Y, it would have been a ten-second swim. But *now*, but *here* — a distance marathon.

"Will!" Luke's voice was breathless, unsteady.

Nothing.

And then his flailing arm smacked right into it — a six-foot piece of the *Phoenix*'s cabin top, floating in the water. The corner glowed like hot coals. Luke used his weight to submerge the smoldering portion. With a puff of steam, the fire was out. He hauled himself on top and lay back, gasping.

"Ow!" His head banged against something hard. He rolled over to find himself staring at a steel-gray smoke-head vent. This was the galley ceiling! It must have been broken off and thrown free when the explosion launched the stove overboard. That's why it was still in one piece when most of the deck and cabin had been blown to toothpicks.

"Will!" he called again with growing urgency.

The *Phoenix* was completely engulfed in flames now. As he watched, a large charred section of stern broke off and disappeared below the waves. The rest of the schooner resettled herself, rocking to and fro into a new balance. Could there be anybody alive on there? Surely he wasn't the only one left?

"Will!" he bellowed. "Lyssa! Ian! Charla!" A pause. "J.J.!" He'd even be happy to see J.J. at this point.

"Luke!"

It was Will. No question about it this time. Careful not to lose his balance on the cabin top, Luke rose to his knees. It was almost completely dark now.

Then he saw it — a flailing arm. He stood up — did he dare stand up? There, twenty yards away, someone — Will? — was rolling in and out of the waves, clinging desperately to a mangled deck plank.

Luke flung himself back on his stomach and began to paddle. He looked up. Will wasn't an inch closer. Here in the open ocean, the wave action canceled out whatever progress he could manage. To save Will, he would have to swim for it.

Swim for it? Was he nuts? He was weak — could hardly force his arms into a dog paddle. A few minutes ago, he'd barely made it to the cabin top ten feet away. This was five times that distance — at least! And the same again coming back, dragging Will, who might be hurt or burned. It was insanity. He'd drown the both of them.

"I can't hang on much longer!" Will called.

The decision was made. A slim chance was better than no chance at all. Luke threw himself off the cabin top and hit the water. He drove each stroke deep into the waves, fighting the sea and his own exhaustion. His eyes stung from salt, but he forced himself to keep them open. *Can't lose him. Can't lose him.* He tried to call Will's name and came up choking on seawater.

Alone! Where was Will? Oh, no! He'd lost Will and — a frantic look backward — he could no longer see the floating cabin top!

He'd given up his raft — his one chance at survival — for nothing.

And then a wave broke, and Luke saw him, still clinging to the piece of deck —

"Will?" Luke blurted.

The boy's face was completely blackened with soot.

Will blinked in amazement. "Luke?" In that instant, Luke realized he must look the same.

He struggled to focus his racing mind on what was important. "Can you swim?"

"I — I'm not sure." Will seemed aimless and confused. "I found a piece of wood — "

"Hang on to it," Luke commanded. "It'll help us float."

Grabbing Will Red Cross style — oh, how he wished he'd paid better attention in that lifesaving class! — Luke started back in the direction of the cabin top. *We'll find it,* he told himself. If they didn't, they would both drown. Sidestroke — shuttle-kick. Will's deadweight threatened to drag him down.

"There's a cabin top floating up ahead," Luke managed to say between tortured breaths. His paddling arm throbbed with pain. "Can you see it?"

"Too dark," replied Will. He sounded sleepy.

"*Try!*" Luke demanded, wasting precious strength shaking his friend. "It's around here somewhere! It has to be!"

"There's nothing," insisted Will, a little more alertly.

Agony pulsed from every muscle in Luke's body, from his cramped feet to the aching knuckles that were locked on to Will's shoulder. It would be so easy to give up right now. There would be no disgrace in that. Who could have expected him to make it this far? The call to quit radiated from the very core of his being. *Just let go,* it seemed to say, *and surrender to the waves . . .*

SHIPWRECK

"Wait a minute," came Will's voice. "What's that?"

Luke kicked like he had never kicked before, as if he had reached down and opened a hidden supply of emergency energy. He screamed as he swam — from pain and rage but mostly from sheer effort.

Whump! His head knocked against something.

"This is it!" he exclaimed. "Will, we found it!"

Luke pushed Will, plank and all, onto the cabin top. Then he scrambled on himself and collapsed, choking and gasping.

"The others? Lyssa?" asked Will.

Luke could only shake his head.

"*Nobody?*"

They turned to face the *Phoenix.* It was a floating bonfire. White-hot flames covered every inch of the schooner except the very peak of the foremast. The bow, which had hung so low, was now pointed up like a cannon as water flooded into the ruined stern.

"They abandoned ship," said Will. "They *must* have!"

Using the deck plank as an oar, Luke paddled alongside the doomed ship, looking for a path through the burning gasoline that coated the sea.

"Hey!" came a voice. "Over here!"

"Where?" chorused Luke and Will. It was pitch-dark now. The fire was the only light on the moonless night.

Suddenly, Luke saw a faint glimmer of canvas struggling through the waves. And attached to it —

"Ian!" Luke cried. "Drop that sail!"

"We need it!" Ian insisted, panting along.

"For *what*?"

Luke and Will almost capsized hauling Ian onto their raft. The younger boy was ready to sink to the bottom of the ocean rather than let go of a large piece of half-charred foresail and a yellow rubber rain hat. Quickly, Luke rolled to the far end of the cabin top to restore balance. The raft wobbled dangerously for a moment and stabilized.

"Where are the others?" rasped Luke.

Ian shrugged helplessly. "I was with J.J., but we got separated."

"What about my sister?" demanded Will.

"I thought she was with you."

"She *was*!" Will was frantic. "But she disappeared in the explosion!"

"And Charla?" asked Luke.

"Charla's — I mean she *was* — " Ian's eyes fell on the flaming hulk of the *Phoenix*. "Oh, God!"

With an audible groan, the burning schooner seemed to give up the fight before their very eyes. Slowly — agonizingly slowly — the ship slid into the sea, following the angle of its raised bow. A split second before it disappeared beneath the waves, a dark shape plunged off the tip of the foremast.

It was a desperation dive, yet it was *perfect*. A graceful arc, and then the slim figure slipped into the ocean with barely a splash. It could have only been one person.

"Charla!" they chorused.

Pointing straight up to the sky, the flaming bowsprit of the *Phoenix* sank out of sight. CNC's schooner was no more. There was a mournful hiss as the ocean extinguished the blazing wreck. Suddenly, all light was gone, save for the few patches of burning gasoline.

Luke picked up the plank and began paddling toward the spot where the girl had entered the water. "Charla!"

"I hope she knows to splash around and make noise," Ian said. "Style counts for nothing when you're being rescued."

They made their way through the gloom, bellowing her name.

"Over here!" She was plowing through the waves in a textbook freestyle.

Luke had to smile. "Maybe we can tie her to the raft and she'll tow us home."

The light mood didn't last long. As they heaved Charla on board, the cabin top overbalanced, flipping them all into the water. Several more tries gave the same result.

"It's too much weight!" Ian shouted, treading water. "This thing won't hold more than three of us!"

"What are we supposed to do?" asked Charla, her voice shrill with panic. "Go eeny-meeny, and the loser drowns?"

"Nobody's going to drown!" panted Luke. "You three climb on; I'll hang off the side!"

Charla was aghast. "Are you crazy? You're shark bait!"

"We'll switch every few hours," Luke decided. "It's only going to get more crowded when we find the others." He cupped his hands to his mouth. "Lyssa! J.J.!"

But his calls went unanswered. And when the last of the gasoline had burned itself out, the cabin top bobbed and rolled in a silent world of limitless black.

CHAPTER SIXTEEN
Tuesday, July 18, 0700 hours

Morning found the makeshift raft still adrift in the middle of nowhere. Luke, Will, and Ian slept the sleep of the exhausted side by side on the tight cabin top. Only Charla, who hung in the water, was awake. She scanned the dawn-gray waves, hoping against hope for some sign of Lyssa and J.J.

Nothing. Less than nothing. No debris from the *Phoenix* — not even a toothpick.

She checked Ian's *National Geographic Explorer* watch — a cheap mail-order thing, but hey, it was the only one that still worked.

Gently, she shook Will's arm. "Will, wake up."

"Lyssa?" murmured Will.

"No, it's me. Your turn for shark-bait position."

"It's the middle of the night," he complained.

"It's seven A.M. Two hours, same as always."

"No fair," grumbled Will, sliding himself over the side.

The switch had to be made carefully to avoid flipping over, but after the long night, they were getting better at it. Charla squeezed herself gingerly on board. Before she lay down, she got her

ISLAND

first real look at the cabin top. It was the galley roof, all right, just like Luke had said. The name of the *Phoenix* had been painted there. Now all that remained were three letters: NIX.

A rueful laugh escaped her lips.

Luke opened a bleary eye. "What?"

She pointed. "We're the *S.S. Nix*."

"It figures," he groaned. "Come on, get some sleep."

But as the tropical sun rose higher and higher in the cloudless sky, sleep became difficult and finally impossible. On board the *Phoenix*, the sails had provided comfortable shade. Now the blazing heat was almost unbearable.

That's when Ian explained why he had risked his life to save a charred piece of the foresail. "It's sun protection," he explained. "We dip it in the water and then pull it over us. See?"

Luke had to admit it was a lot cooler under the dripping canvas. He repositioned the scrap of sail so that it covered Charla, who was once again in the shark-bait spot.

"What's the hat for?" asked Will.

"To collect rain," replied Ian. "It's rubber, so it won't leak. We can't drink the ocean water because of the salt. We need freshwater."

Charla was amazed. "How did you think of all this in the middle of a burning boat?"

Ian shrugged. "I once saw this show on ship-wrecks on the Discovery Channel. The big difference between who survived and who didn't was thirst and sunburn."

"Geez, that's smart," commented Will. "I sure hope Lyssa thought of that when she — I mean, *if . . .*" His voice trailed off.

"Did anybody see her last night?" asked Luke.

"No, not Lyssa," Charla said slowly. "I remember J.J. trapped on the foredeck. But once the sail caught fire, I lost him in the smoke."

"I was with him for a few seconds," Ian added. "Then the mast came down and we got split up. But he was definitely okay. I heard him calling for me."

"Did you see him after that?" asked Luke.

Ian shook his head. "But I don't think he went down with the ship. I mean, the heat was unbelievable. The fire was spreading — there was nowhere to stand. Sooner or later, he would have had to jump."

Charla looked alarmed. "Then why didn't we see him in the water? Or at least hear him? And what about Lyssa?"

There was a sober silence, broken only by the *slap, slap* of the water lapping at the wooden platform.

Then Will spoke. "Aw, Lyss, I knew you'd bust it."

Luke gazed at him in concern. "Will? You okay?"

"That's the last thing I said to her," he replied quietly. "She rebuilt the engine on guts alone, and that was the thanks she got from me."

Nobody could offer a single word of comfort.

Will looked out over the miles of empty sea. *I should have been an only child.* How many times had he said it? How many more had he thought it? And now . . .

If Lyssa's okay, he vowed, *I'll —*

Automatically, his mind sorted through the dozens of promises he might offer up. Suddenly, they all seemed so meaningless — a collection of tacky New Year's resolutions.

He finally settled on the one he feared he might not get the chance to make good on:

If Lyssa's okay, I'll never be mean to her again.

SHIPWRECK

CHAPTER SEVENTEEN
Wednesday, July 19, 0030 hours

Night was the worst. The darkness closed in like an endless canopy of absolute blackness. With no moon, Luke couldn't even see Charla a few inches away.

"Ian, what time is it?" came Will's voice from the void.

"It's twelve-thirty," Luke said irritably. "We just checked two minutes ago."

"I don't really care about the time. I just want to see the light." He was talking about the tiny light on Ian's watch. "Every time I fall asleep, I dream that I've gone blind. I need to see something."

"Try looking at the stars," suggested Ian from the water beside the raft.

"I can't sleep on my back."

Luke was growing impatient. "You might have noticed this isn't the Hilton. Make do."

As Will struggled to roll over, he kneed Charla in the thigh. Reacting in shock, she elbowed Luke in the ribs. And as he jackknifed in pain, the edge of the raft dipped, dunking Ian underwater. The tiniest move had a ripple effect through the whole

ISLAND

group. It was that close and uncomfortable.

Sputtering, Ian checked his watch. "Twelve-thirty-three," he reported.

"Do it again. I missed it," said Will.

Although the temperature never dropped below seventy degrees, the night felt almost bone-chilling after the burning heat of the day. Taking turns in shark-bait position kept the castaways soaked to the skin, and the six-hour shifts out of the water did little to dry them off. The seas had picked up, and even the smallest waves washed over the cabin top.

They had tried again to find an arrangement where all four of them could sit on the raft at the same time. But after repeated dunkings and one real scare — the raft had almost bobbed away — they had decided that three riders and one shark bait was the only way to go.

Secretly, Luke didn't mind his shifts in the water, especially at night. While the air cooled down, the ocean stayed warm. It also provided protection from the wind. In fact, the only problem with shark-bait position was exactly what the name implied: sharks. Dangling there, you were a sitting duck for any sea creature that wanted to take a bite.

They had seen fins cutting the surface around the raft, but Ian insisted they were dolphins. "A shark fin is larger and more triangular, with a small slot near the bottom."

The kid was an endless fountain of information that nobody wanted to hear. "*Carcharadon carcharias*, the great white shark, could destroy this raft in a single bite. A really big specimen can swallow a person whole."

"Let me guess," said Will. "They did sharks on *National Geographic Explorer*."

"Don't knock it," mumbled Luke. "Those guys make one heck of a watch."

"I'm more afraid of the tiger shark," Ian went on seriously. "They're pack hunters and they can go into what's called a 'feeding frenzy — ' "

"Enough," interrupted Charla, who was in shark-bait position at the time. "I don't want to hear another word about it until *you're* hanging down here like a worm on a hook."

With the heat of the second day came thirst — thirst beyond anything they had experienced before in their lives. It was a familiar feeling at first — like the desire to hit the water fountain after a long boring class on a steamy June afternoon. But then it transformed into something deeper and stronger. There was no water fountain; there never would be. Throats burned. Lips cracked and bled.

Charla held the empty rubber hat. "Did that show about shipwrecks mention what to do if it doesn't rain?" she asked Ian.

"It'll rain," the boy promised.

The other three noticed, though, that this was one statement with no backup research from television.

There was hunger too — they hadn't eaten for a full forty-eight hours. The hunger mingled with the thirst to produce a never-ending dull ache that gripped each survivor from head to toe. It was a pain that radiated lack — lack of water, lack of food, lack of sleep, lack of comfort.

As the afternoon progressed, a few clouds appeared overhead. The castaways cheered them on as if the Super Bowl were being played out in the sky above them. A cool wind picked up, creating a chop on top of the water.

"All right, rain!" croaked Will. "Let's see what you've got!"

"We should trap water in the sail and drink it as it runs over the sides," Ian lectured. "Get as much as you can while it's still raining, because the hat won't hold a lot."

Luke had his hands out, palms up, waiting for the downpour.

It didn't come. Or, at least, not to them. They could see it raining a quarter-mile ahead of them, but they didn't get a single drop. There was genuine agony on the cabin top when the overcast thinned out and the sun broke through once again.

"No fair!" Will moaned, addressing the clouds. "Come back! Come back! Where's our rain?"

That night, Luke hung over the side, drifting in and out of an uneasy world of half-dreams. You never really slept in shark-bait position for fear of slipping off the raft and being lost forever. Suddenly, he heard a strange gurgling noise. It sounded like — drinking?

Will had edged his way forward and was now lying with his head over the side, swallowing greedily.

Aghast, Luke grabbed him by the collar and pulled his face out of the water. "Don't do that, Will! It's suicide!"

It was so dark that all Luke could see were Will's eyes. They seemed dazed, glassy, and feverish. "It's water, man! Who cares if there's salt in it?"

Luke shook him angrily. "That salt dehydrates you worse than going thirsty. You might have just cut a whole day off the time you can hold out! Maybe more!"

"No, it's okay!" Will insisted urgently. "Listen,

I figured out why we never found Lyssa and J.J. — they've been rescued already!"

"It doesn't make sense, Will," Luke argued. "How could rescuers spot them and miss us?"

"J.J. was right all along!" Will explained. "The captain and Radford are watching us! The others were in trouble, so they moved in and saved them. They haven't saved us yet because we're doing okay."

"Okay?" Luke repeated. "You call this okay? We're starving — *dying* of thirst! One of us has to hang in the water or we all drown. *Think!* A shark could bite me in two this minute, and the rescue boat would get here in time to save three and a half people. There *is* no bigger trouble than what we're in right now. If there were rescuers out there, they'd be rescuing us!"

Will looked at him pityingly. "Take it easy, Luke. Everything's under control. Don't panic."

Luke stared back at him in growing horror. The kid was totally serious. There was only one explanation for this: Hunger, thirst, grief, and fear were causing Will Greenfield to lose his grip on reality.

How long would it be before the same thing happened to the rest of them?

CHAPTER EIGHTEEN
Thursday, July 20, 1645 hours

When it finally rained, everybody was unprepared. Luke and Charla both pulled the sail canvas in opposite directions, spilling most of the water onto the raft, where it rolled off into the sea. Will had the shakes and the dry heaves from drinking salt water. He tried to stand up and catch the drops in his cupped hands but succeeded only in tumbling off the cabin top headfirst into the ocean. By the time they managed to haul him back on board, the tropical cloudburst was over. The rain hat held about an inch and a half of water. It was enough for two mouthfuls each.

The water was warm and tasted a little salty — the rain hat, along with the raft and everything on it, was crusted with sea salt. But it was freshwater — their first in three days.

"Every little bit helps," muttered Luke in disgust. "What a joke! It's better to have nothing than a thimbleful."

"This was just enough to remind us how much we need and we're not getting," Charla agreed mournfully.

Will's stomach was in such bad shape that he

couldn't even keep his share down. He took one gulp and spit up over the side.

The other three looked on in agony. To them, nothing could be sadder than the thought of wasted water.

Boredom became as much of a problem as hunger and thirst. Minutes rolled into hours, which rolled into days with a dreary gray sameness. The overwhelming dullness canceled out every other emotion — even, at last, fear. It teamed up with the body's weakness to sink Luke into an almost sleepy fog.

A couple of days before, his every thought had been of rescue. Now it seldom crossed his mind. He didn't expect to be rescued; sometimes he was so numb that he couldn't have cared less whether he was rescued or not. There were moments when the Coast Guard could have rearended the cabin top and he probably wouldn't even have noticed.

He could tell he wasn't the only one. By the next day, Will had virtually stopped talking. He lay on his side under the damp sail, his parched lips slightly apart, drifting in and out of a light doze. If anyone spoke to him, he only answered about half the time. More often than not, his replies made no sense at all.

When Ian informed Will that it was his turn for shark-bait position, he was told, "You know, Lyssa came in second in chess club, but she lost to Seth Birnbaum in the final."

By unspoken agreement, Luke, Ian, and Charla stopped asking Will to take his turn dangling in the ocean. One thing was obvious: If they spent much more time lost at sea, Will was not going to survive.

From the start, Charla had stubbornly insisted on exercising, doing aquatics, and taking short swims during her shark-bait time. Now she hung off the edge of the raft, gazing at the horizon with vacant eyes and never making an unnecessary move.

Of the four of them, only Ian seemed to have the energy to talk. He filled the endless hours with a tedious monologue of every single detail he knew about the ocean. And he knew plenty.

"Hey, Ian," mumbled Luke listlessly. "Don't you think it's time to close up the Encyclopedia Boronica and give us all a break?"

The boy flushed redder than his harsh sun- and wind-burn. "I talk too much," he said sadly. "I'm boring."

"I was just kidding." Luke was instantly sorry. "If it wasn't for you and the Discovery Channel, we'd be dead already. Talk all you like."

"I shouldn't," Ian conceded. "When you talk, the moisture inside your mouth evaporates, and you get dehydrated faster."

"Man," sighed Luke, "I'd give anything for a Gameboy. Or even a lousy deck of cards."

"I'd settle for a piece of string," Charla put in. "I used to know how to do Cat's Cradle."

"A lot of people don't know that blue whales are bigger than sperm whales." Ian took up his lecture. "They said on TV once that a blue whale's tongue weighs as much as an elephant."

"Ian — " Luke groaned.

"Seriously," the boy continued earnestly. "Look at that one over there. It must be thirty yards long."

Luke sat up in sudden surprise. "What one over where?"

"The whale," Ian insisted. "He's spouting water twenty feet high."

Luke stared. Before them the Pacific Ocean stretched, blue-gray and unbroken, to the horizon. There was no whale. He exchanged a worried glance with Charla and turned back to the younger boy.

"In that show about shipwrecks," he asked carefully, "what were the warning signs? I mean, how do you know when you're not going to make it?"

"Slow, lazy behavior," Ian replied. "Too much sleeping. Followed by hallucinations — people see things that aren't really there." He pointed. "Look — he's spouting again."

CHAPTER NINETEEN
Sunday, July 23, 1320 hours

Sun.

Luke was aware of its harsh glare even through closed eyes. He could feel the pain of sunburn on his face and arms.

But no. This wasn't right. There was supposed to be protection. Something white. A large sheet — a sail? Where was his corner?

He spoke to the others. *Cover me up, here. I'm getting fried.* Funny — why couldn't he hear his own voice? *Come on, guys.* This time he held his hand to his mouth. His lips weren't moving either. His brain was talking, but it didn't seem to be connected to his tongue.

He had been in shark-bait position for two — three — how many days now? He would have loved to stretch out and sleep.

Hey, Charla, he tried to say. *Your turn.*

Was she ignoring him? No, his mouth was still not working. He couldn't expect people to read his mind — especially not unconscious people. And they were. All three of them.

Will had been first, even before their second rainstorm. They'd forced water down his throat, but it hadn't revived him. And anyway, Ian and Charla had gone down the very next day. Poor Ian. None of them deserved this, but the little kid was the most innocent of them all, guilty of nothing more than watching too much TV. Now here he lay, with a bird perched on his head.

A bird?

No, that couldn't be right. Luke's eyes were playing tricks on him again. There were no birds out here in the open ocean. They had to stay within flying range of land.

He'd been having a lot of hallucinations. Like a couple of hours ago — days ago? — when he'd had a very clear memory of Reese stashing that gun in his locker. Crazy! How could he remember what he hadn't seen? Of course, he *knew* it had been Reese, even though the jerk denied it. So Luke's hazy mind had put together what must have happened and constructed a fake memory out of it.

It was not very different from Ian's whale — the beginning of the end.

It was a terrible end, Luke decided, because your last thought is the one where you realize you're losing your mind.

What was this? His body wriggled with revulsion as a long slimy shape attacked and wrapped itself around his neck. He let go of the raft and tore at it, ripping it to pieces. An eel? The tentacle of a giant squid? Through the fog of his confusion, he struggled to focus on what was in his hands.

Seaweed. Another hallucination. There was no seaweed in the open ocean either.

Splashing wildly, he managed to regain his grip on the raft. He had no idea why he was struggling so hard to preserve his doomed life a few extra minutes. What was the point? They were all dead, courtesy of Rat-face.

Rat-face — what a waste of a thought when there weren't many thoughts left.

Luke forced the mate's picture out of his brain. But its replacement image was too painful — a fleeting glimpse of his parents, who would mourn him. He closed his eyes tightly, but they were still there.

Make this stop! he tried to exclaim.

And when he opened his eyes again, he saw the fin.

Another hallucination?

Maybe, but this one struck him right in the ribs.

Shark! He tried to sound the warning, but the technical difficulties between his brain and his mouth still existed.

The raft bobbed away from the fin. Luke held

his breath. The long shape in the water followed.

Another bump! Luke braced himself for the ripping, tearing bite that was to come next. But when he looked down, he saw the bottle-nosed snout of a dolphin.

This time it nudged the raft, and Luke was pulled along. He remembered somewhere in Ian's rambling lecture stories of dolphins pushing drowning sailors to safety. Surely this was the final hallucination, the last desperate brain impulses of a dying mind. He was amazed at how vivid it was — the white water roaring around him, the pounding of surf, the sudden thump of his dangling feet onto shallow sandy bottom.

Instinct took over — instinct and a frantic desire to die on dry land. Luke pushed the raft with every ounce of strength that remained in his exhausted body — kept on pushing, even when the cabin top dug into the beach and would move no more.

CHAPTER TWENTY
Sunday, July 23, 1555 hours

It was a drenching rain, a downpour, a deluge. As Luke slept, he dreamed that hundreds of tiny jackhammers were working on his face. The water quickly puddled up in his eye sockets and in the hollows on both sides of his nose. The trickle found his lips.

Water. Real water. Drinking water.

He sat bolt upright and stared around him in confusion. Palm trees. Jungle. A sandy beach.

He leaped up too fast, toppling over and landing in the surf. As he lay there in the shallows, an amazing sight met his eyes. The cabin top was jammed into the heavy sand just above the tide line. Will, Charla, and Ian lay upon it, still unconscious. Between Ian and Charla sat the rain hat, propped up by their bodies and full to overflowing with freshwater.

Luke crawled through the surf, bent over the raft, and stuck his head into the hat, drinking greedily. Nothing had ever tasted better. He could have happily remained there, draining the hat dry. It took a gigantic effort to pull himself away.

SHIPWRECK

Carefully, like he was handling nitro, he picked up the hat and held it to Will's cracked lips.

Luke watched the precious water roll down Will's chin. Finally, a tiny amount managed to find its way into his mouth. It dribbled down the back of his throat; he choked suddenly. Poor Will still couldn't keep anything down.

He moved on to Charla. He propped her up on the sand and began by wetting her lips with water from his finger. The girl opened her eyes and her mouth at the same time.

"Where — ?"

"Drink," Luke interrupted.

And she did, gulping so deeply that she ended up choking too, although not a drop was wasted.

The two attended to Ian. The younger boy smacked his lips at the first taste. Then he swallowed and kept on swallowing. He sat up, grabbed the hat, and chug-a-lugged.

In the spot where he had been lying, the raft still said NIX.

"Save some for Will," ordered Luke.

Charla looked worried, still disoriented. "I don't know," she said nervously. "Will's really messed up. He hasn't moved in days."

Luke spilled water on Will's upturned face and forced some past the parched lips. The boy choked again, but this time the water stayed down. Luke dropped to his knees and gently slapped Will's cheeks. "Come on, Will. Join the party."

No response.

All three hunkered down and tried everything they could think of to rouse their friend. No amount of shaking, pinching, chafing, and massaging had any effect.

"He's definitely alive," concluded Ian, "but there's no telling when he'll snap out of it. It could be five minutes from now; it could be never." He flushed at Luke's angry look and explained, "I saw it on the Learning Channel."

Charla looked around. "What *is* this place?"

"Who cares?" Luke replied. "It *isn't* the raft. It's land, and that's all that matters."

"It must be an island," mused Ian. "There's no way we could have drifted far enough to reach continental land. This is a miracle! To hit an island in this part of the Pacific is as unlikely as two bullets striking each other head-on. We lucked out."

"Luck had nothing to do with it," said Luke. "It was that dolphin."

SHIPWRECK

They stared at him. "Dolphin?" repeated Charla.

"You must have seen it," Luke insisted. "It pushed us in to the island. Just like you told us, Ian. Dolphins try to help people. This one saved our lives."

"You must have been hallucinating," Ian said kindly. "There wasn't any dolphin. A big wind blew us here. Don't you remember? One minute we were drifting, and the next we were being carried along by a hot wind. It felt sort of like the dryer in a car wash."

"You're both crazy!" exclaimed Charla. "Nothing brought us here. We swam in. We lined up along the raft and kicked like crazy. When I close my eyes, I can still see us doing it."

They stared at one another, bewildered, as the rain beat down.

Ian seemed to choose his words very carefully. "I think maybe we're *all* right — inside our minds."

By that time, the rubber hat was full again. Charla drank some more and passed it around.

Luke raised it like a champagne glass. "To *us*, man! I can't believe we made it!" His face fell suddenly. "And to those who didn't make it."

It was a painful thought, one that packed the wallop of a sledgehammer. But the castaways had more pressing problems — the need for food, the need for shelter, the need to help their unconscious friend. So they set aside their grieving and made plans to explore the island that had risen from the sea to save their lives.

ABOUT THE AUTHOR

GORDON KORMAN is the author of more than thirty-five books for children and young adults, including most recently *The Chicken Doesn't Skate*, the Slapshots series, and *Liar, Liar, Pants on Fire*. He lives in Long Island with his wife and son. Although he has never been stranded on a desert island, he did a lot of research to write this, his first adventure novel.